# CENSORED BY CONFUCIUS

NEW STUDIES IN ASIAN CULTURE

# CENSORED BY CONFUCIUS

## Ghost Stories

by Yuan Mei

Edited and Translated with an Introduction by

Kam Louie and

Louise Edwards

An East Gate Book

LONDON AND NEW YORK

**An East Gate Book**

First published 1996 by M.E. Sharpe

Published 2015 by Routledge
2 Park Square, Milton Park, Abingdon, Oxon OX14 4RN
711 Third Avenue, New York, NY 10017, USA

*Routledge is an imprint of the Taylor & Francis Group, an informa business*

Copyright © 1996 Taylor & Francis. All rights reserved.

No part of this book may be reprinted or reproduced or utilised in any form or by any electronic, mechanical, or other means, now known or hereafter invented, including photocopying and recording, or in any information storage or retrieval system, without permission in writing from the publishers.

Notices
No responsibility is assumed by the publisher for any injury and/or damage to persons or property as a matter of products liability, negligence or otherwise, or from any use of operation of any methods, products, instructions or ideas contained in the material herein.

Practitioners and researchers must always rely on their own experience and knowledge in evaluating and using any information, methods, compounds, or experiments described herein. In using such information or methods they should be mindful of their own safety and the safety of others, including parties for whom they have a professional responsibility.

Product or corporate names may be trademarks or registered trademarks, and are used only for identification and explanation without intent to infringe.

**Library of Congress Cataloging-in-Publication Data**

Yüan, Mei, 1716–1798.
[Tzu pu yü. English]
Censored by Confucius: ghost stories by Yuan Mei / edited and translated by Kam Louie and Louise Edwards.
p. cm.
"East Gate book"
ISBN 1-56324-680-5 (alk. paper).
ISBN 1-56324-681-3 (alk. paper pbk.)
ISBN-13 978-1-56324-681-4 (alk. paper pbk.)

I. Louie, Kam. II. Edwards, Louise, 1962–
III. Title.
PL2735.A5T913 1995
895.1'34—dc20 95-34203
CIP

ISBN 13: 9781563246814 (pbk)
ISBN 13: 9781563246807 (hbk)

*For Chris and Alex*

隨園先生像

*Yuan Mei*

# *Contents*

# *List of Stories by Theme*

## Animals



## Fox Fairies



## Ghostly Revenge

**Homosexuality**



**Incubi**

**Legal Cases**

*Human World*



*Underworld*



**Lovers**

**Military**



**Monks and Nuns**



**Natural Phenomena and Strange Lands**

**Physical Transformations**



**Prostitutes and Widows**



**Scholars**

**Sex**

**Subduing Ghosts**



**Theft**

# *Illustrations*

# *Preface*

As one of the most famous Chinese scholars of the eighteenth century, Yuan Mei offered especially valuable insights into life and society in Qing China. The stories in this volume provide a vision of how the trials and tribulations of a wide cross-section of the citizens were understood and resolved. Rituals surrounding the belief in ghosts played an important part in the lives of the Chinese, and yet the manner in which these beliefs were practiced is often not fully appreciated. Confucian-influenced scholarship has tended to avoid matters such as ghosts, sex, and crime, preferring to direct the reader's attention to the weighty matters of self-cultivation and government. But, as the stories in this volume clearly demonstrate, popular culture and popular religion thrive beyond the elite moral strictures found in Confucian texts.

The first table of contents follows the order of the stories as they appeared in Yuan Mei's text. We have also provided a thematic table of contents with the aim of helping readers target tales of more personal interest. We hope this volume will prove useful to a wide range of students of China and its literature, anthropology, and history, as well as to the general reader of ghost stories.

We would like to thank the following people for their help and advice: Bing Leung, George Joshua, Rod Bucknell, Kath Filmer-Davies, Jill Reid, Judy Glasgow, Yew-jin Fang, Malcom Skewis, and Doug Merwin and his production team at M.E. Sharpe.

Kam Louie
University of Queensland

Louise Edwards
Australian Catholic University
April 1995, Brisbane

# *Introduction*

Yuan Mei's controversial collection of short tales of the strange and supernatural, *Censored by Confucius*, first appeared in 1788,[1] only ten years before Yuan's death. Written in a climate of political and moral conservativism fostered by stifling Confucian orthodoxy, these tales of ghosts, sex, betrayal, revenge, litigation, transvestism, homosexuality, and corruption provide a rich tableau of daily life in China. The popularity of these "exposés" led to their censorship in 1836 as the Qing government (1644–1911) attempted to control the spread of anti-establishment sentiment (Chan 1991, p. 40). Yuan Mei scorned the prudery and moralism propagated by the court and orthodox Confucian scholars of his time, choosing instead to expose hypocrisy and excessive puritanism as the real problems of mid-Qing society.

His direct challenge to court orthodoxy in these tales is reflected in the title he chose for the collection. The phrase "censored by Confucius" (*zi bu yu*) is drawn from the seventh book of the Confucian *Analects—Zi bu yu guai, li, luan, shen.* This has been variously translated as "The subjects on which the Master did not talk, were extraordinary things, feats of strength, disorder, and spiritual beings" (Legge 1985, p. 201); "The topics the Master did not speak of were prodigies, force, disorder and gods" (Lau 1982, p. 88); and "The Master never talked of wonders, feats of strength, disorders of nature, or spirits" (Waley 1956, p. 120).

Thus, where the official, Confucian-inspired version of Qing life and culture finds the supernatural and the immoderate anathema, Yuan Mei found them to be a rich and challenging source of inspiration. Moreover, his impolitic citation of "the Master" did not pass unnoticed by his contemporaries. Zhang Xuecheng, a conservative scholar by comparison with Yuan, gained fame for his savage invectives against the "heretical" Yuan's use of classic Confucian texts:

> . . . there has never been anyone [except Yuan Mei] who, in broad daylight and beneath the warming sun, has dared to go to this extreme in denying the precedence of the Classics, doing away with sanctity and law, and indulging in such perverse, depraved, obscene, and licentious ideas! (cited in Nivison 1966, p. 264)[2]

For his part, Yuan justifies his unconventional collection as the whims of an aging man who wishes to spend his remaining days as enjoyably as possible. In his "Seven Poems on Aging" he writes of the many pleasures he finds in his increasing years:

> Talk of books—why they please or fail to please—
> Or of ghosts and marvels, no matter how far-fetched,
> These are excesses in which, should he feel inclined,
> A man of seventy-odd may well indulge. (cited in Birch 1972, p. 199)

While Confucius may not have condoned discussion of ghosts and marvels, lust and love, crime and retribution, Yuan and a large section of the reading public most certainly did. Arthur Waley writes of the collection, "The Chinese had an insatiable appetite for wonder-tales, and collections of them had been made since very early times" (Waley 1956, p. 120). Having established himself in the previous half century as one of the greatest poets of his era, a prodigy in scholarship, and a formidable literary critic, Yuan was more than confident enough to indulge his literary whims as a septuagenarian.

His satisfaction with the collection and his enjoyment of the reaction it drew are evident in his continuation of the task. In 1796, a mere two years before his death, he completed a sequel—his increasing age perhaps inspiring his continued interest in the life of the underworld and its interaction with the living.

## The Life of Yuan Mei

Yuan Mei's life was both long and immensely successful. He was born in 1716 in Hangzhou, a city famous for its beautiful scenery and rich literary tradition. His family was genteel but rather poor. His father took up junior secretarial positions around the country as a means of support. Yuan began his formal schooling at six and progressed so rapidly that by the age of eleven he had passed the first-level examinations and become an accredited scholar. For a man, success in Qing society was measured largely in terms of his ability to pass the various levels of official examinations. The degrees thereby conferred granted the scholar access to the range of positions available in the extensive government bureaucracy. Yuan's early success confirmed his reputation as a prodigy—many men spent their whole lives failing the examinations. In 1736, less than a decade after Yuan's initial success, the emperor announced a set of special examinations for selecting scholars to write the official histories. Yuan was selected to represent Hangzhou and at age twenty was the youngest candidate to attend. He was not, however, one of the fifteen, from a total of two hundred aspirants, to pass. His feelings about this failure and the ghostly encounter that preceded it form part of one of the stories in *Censored by Confucius*. In "Memories of Suiyuan" he narrates how the ghost of an old family retainer told him before the examinations that he would not be successful. The enthusiastic and optimistic young Yuan remained unconvinced of this premonition until the results were published.

Yuan spent the next two years perfecting his examination technique while struggling to make ends meet as a tutor for various families of the gentry. In 1738 he at last succeeded in passing the second-level examinations. Then in the following year his career took several major steps forward. He passed not only the third-level examinations but also the Palace Examinations, which secured his admittance as a fellow to the most prestigious national center of learning, the Hanlin Academy. During the winter of this same year, 1739, he was called home by his parents to marry a certain Miss Wang, to whom he had long been engaged. For the next decade Yuan was employed by the throne first as a scholar and then as a bureaucrat.

His first posting, in 1743, was to Lishui, where at age twenty-seven he was appointed prefect. In 1745 he was transferred to the more senior post of prefect in a suburb of Nanjing. Inspiration for many of the tales in this collection undoubtedly developed during these years as an official. His contact with the social problems experienced by average citizens and his awareness of various miscarriages of justice form the basis of many of the tales. The ghostly revenge on corrupt officials depicted therein perhaps reflects a popular fantasy of "just desserts" generated to assuage the sense of powerlessness among the more vulnerable citizens of Qing China. Arthur Waley's biography of Yuan provides many examples of actual judicial cases over which he presided. All these cases reveal Yuan's concern that the law be enforced humanely and without excessive moralism (Waley 1956, pp. 31–43).

By 1749 Yuan had grown weary of official life. He took early retirement at the age of thirty-three intending to continue his life as a poet, critic, and author of considerable stature. Yuan chose as his home a newly purchased property in Nanjing, the Sui Garden.[3] With his excellent reputation as a bureaucrat and his contacts at the highest level of the Manchu court well established, Yuan was not destined to spend his remaining half century in straitened circumstances. He occupied himself composing funeral inscriptions for the deceased relatives of friends and acquaintances, and writing poetry, which was always in high demand. In sum, his retirement ensured him a relatively carefree life that, in its rejection of stifling Confucian moralism, was lively enough to cause unfavorable comment from distinguished figures in the Nanjing area. Two features of his life as a leisured intellectual drew considerable disfavor —his sexual adventures and his attitude toward women's education.

During his employment by the throne, Yuan Mei had led an active social life and developed quite a reputation for loose living. He was well known for his fondness for boy actors and young women, but besides these sexual preferences, which were not entirely uncommon during his lifetime, his general lack of regard for social norms raised more than a few eyebrows in and around Nanjing. One of the sources of income for his retirement was the teaching of poetry writing, and while this in itself could cause no scandal, Yuan included "among his students (this was thought especially outrageous) . . . a fair number of talented ladies" (Nivison 1966, p. 263). His tutorials for women became known collectively as the "moth-eyebrow academy," for it was deemed desirable for beautiful women of the time to acquire mothlike eyebrows. Yuan's poetry-writing classes were held in his own home, the Sui Garden. This was thought particularly scandalous by intellectuals such as Zhang Xuecheng, since young women from wealthy families were normally educated in their own homes and most certainly not in the company of men from outside their immediate families.[4] Yuan's circulation of the poetry written by his female students compounded the affront to conservative social practice for it took the products of the "inner female realm" out into the "public male domain."

Waley translated a mock letter of complaint about Yuan's conduct written by his friend and fellow poet Zhao Yi.

> One of the complaints is that Yuan, having settled in his garden, "ransacked the neighbourhood for whatever was soft and warm, not minding whether it

> was boy or girl." "He entices young ladies of good family to his house," the document goes on, "and all the 'moth-eyebrows' (i.e. handsome girls) are enlisted as his pupils." "He regards himself as stage-manager of all the elegances; but is in reality a sinner against the teachings of Confucius." (Waley 1956, p. 77)

Such outrageous behavior came close to earning Yuan banishment from Nanjing. His attitudes toward pleasure put him at odds not only with many of his Confucian peers but also with his Buddhist friends. Encouraged by Peng Shaosheng (1740–1796) to take up Buddhism, Yuan Mei wrote disdainfully of the Buddhist goal of relinquishing all desires:

> ". . . what makes a live man different from a dead one is precisely that he is capable of enjoying such pleasures." "What you are asking me to do," Yuan Mei continues, "is to behave as though I were dead, when in fact I am not dead." (Waley 1956, p. 82)

Yuan saw no sin in pleasure seeking and clearly intended to live life to the full—uninhibited by moralists who would have much preferred that the Qing dynasty's greatest poet from south of the Yangzi live a sedate life more befitting a man of his talent and reputation.

Yuan Mei spent the remainder of his life in a genteel but indulgent fashion, traveling, collecting recipes, writing poetry, and composing funeral inscriptions.[5] He was interrupted only by the periodic bouts of malaria that had plagued him for decades. He died in his early eighties, survived by two sons (one adopted) and a daughter. Three other daughters died before he was fifty-four, and this may explain his fondness for nurturing the literary skills of young women. In his will he made fun of religious rites and Buddhist monks:

> When I die I would be exceptionally pleased if you would tell your sisters to come mourn for me. I would really loathe religious chanting and vegetarian rites in the wake. If you come to weep for me, I would be greatly moved. But if the monks disturb my spirit by banging their wooden fish drums, I will make a hasty exit with my hands placed firmly over my ears. Would you feel at peace knowing that this had happened? (cited in Yang 1992, p. 247)

## *Biji xiaoshuo*

Yuan Mei is best known for his poetry and literary criticism. His many poems and his essays on poetics celebrate the joys of living one's life as one chooses, without having to imitate or be restricted by the teachings of the ancients. The most singular and significant feature of Yuan's style is its perverse and indulgent streak, almost a literary hedonism, which ensured that his work stood above that of his contemporaries. Lo and Shultz write of his poetic style, "Countering the prevailing demand that poetry must be didactic . . . Yuan held that the function of poetry is to delight" (Lo and Shultz 1986, p. 191). Yuan's *joie de vivre* is reflected also in his love of good food. Known as a gourmet, he wrote many recipes for his favorite dishes (Spence 1977, pp. 259–94).

Yuan Mei's delight in life is also reflected in the short tales represented in this volume. His amoral, amused, and sometimes shockingly frank depiction of everyday life ensured that under his pen the genre of *biji xiaoshuo* would reach new heights. Clearly written with the goal of amusing both himself and his readers, the tales avoid moralism and are always written with wit and wonder at the mysteries of life, death, lust, and crime.

*Biji xiaoshuo,* translated by Y. M. Ma as "note-form literature," have a long history in China (Ma 1986, pp. 650–52). These short classical prose tales first appeared in works of the Six Dynasties (221–590), though the genre may very well extend as far back as the Han (206 B.C.E.–220 C.E.). Distinguished by two main characteristics—brevity and casualness —*biji xiaoshuo,* Ma notes, usually appear as collections rather than independent stories. Covering philology, history, or fiction, *biji xiaoshuo* form a significant part of China's prose heritage.

The earliest *biji,* and the subgenre most directly related to Yuan Mei's tales, are called *zhiguai*—records of the strange and anomalous.[6] The Han dynasty volume *Shan hai jing* (The classic of mountain and seas) is the most famous forerunner of this style of writing. It records strange creatures and semihuman beings living in mythical lands.[7] By the time of the Three Kingdoms and Six Dynasties, *zhiguai* writing had become an important and popular pursuit among the literati. The most highly regarded work of this time, Gan Bao's (fl. 320) *Soushen ji* (In search of the supernatural), is still regarded as a definitive example of this style of writing. The revival and importance of the Daoist alchemists (*fangshi*) during this period, with their search for immortality and other occult goals, may account for the popularity of tales of the supernatural in Wei-Jin times.[8]

By the Tang dynasty (618–907) another subgenre of *biji* had risen to prominence—the *chuanqi. Chuanqi* literally means "recounting the strange." This new narrative form is still characterized by short sketches in the classical language, but the supernatural, where it appears, becomes incidental to more conventional scenes and events. The central characters are typically talented young men and beautiful young women and the plot often involves the resolution of their romantic entanglements.

By the Ming (1368–1644) and Qing dynasties, the *biji xiaoshuo* had integrated both the *zhiguai* and the *chuanqi* traditions, resulting in brilliant collections of tales that combine the supernatural with the romantic. The most famous collection is the *Liaozhai zhiyi* (Strange tales from the leisure studio) by Pu Songling, who died in 1715, one year before Yuan Mei was born. In the West, Pu has enjoyed a long and sympathetic reception as a result of the continued publication of translations of his fiction. As early as 1880 an English translation by Herbert Giles of a selection of stories from the *Liaozhai zhiyi* was published, and later translators have rendered Pu's work into a variety of other languages. The popularity of Pu's *biji* ghost stories has therefore been assured not only in China but also internationally.[9] Yuan Mei and Ji Yun (1724–1805), probably the most accomplished and well known of the generation of writers after Pu, were also masters of the *biji* style. Indeed, during their own lifetimes Yuan and Ji were already so accomplished that they were celebrated in the expression *nan Yuan bei Ji* ("Yuan in the south and Ji in the north"). The absence of a comprehensive English translation of Yuan's *biji xiaoshuo* has clearly hindered promotion of his writings in the English-speaking world.[10] Although Yuan is more famous for his poetry than his *biji xiaoshuo* and Ji is known primarily for his compilation of the *Siku quanshu* (Complete library of four branches of books),[11] both writers made significant contributions to the *biji* genre.

While Pu, Ji, and Yuan are often regarded as the greatest storytellers of the Qing dynasty, there are differences in their tales. These may be explained in part by the authors' different life histories. Unlike Pu, who was impoverished all his life, Yuan and Ji mixed with the wealthiest and most influential of the age and enjoyed official recognition of their talent within in the Qing bureaucracy. Both owe more to the *zhiguai* of the earlier dynasties than to the *chuanqi,* which Pu freely imitated. As a consequence, Yuan's *biji* stories are more dense and the language less colloquial, and indeed more classical in style. They were clearly intended for an educated reader's own pleasure rather than for public readings. Pu uses his fiction to vent his frustration and Ji uses his ghost stories to preach that virtue is rewarded and evil punished. While these sentiments can also be found in Yuan's tales, the resentment and didacticism found in the works of the other two are mostly absent (Shen 1988, p. 2).

## *Censored by Confucius*: Main Themes

*Censored by Confucius* contains a number of recurring themes. Besides giving insight into Yuan Mei's artistic talent, these themes provide a wealth of information about life in the mid-Qing. Collected over a lengthy period, these stories purport to be actual events recorded by Yuan. The full range of life experiences, from family tensions through natural disasters, can all be accounted for by the existence of a supernatural realm. Some of Yuan's tales are full of jest and good humor; others leave the reader with a sense of revulsion. But they are always witty and unpredictable. Both the moral and mystical orders that suffused the society in which Yuan lived are apparent throughout. The world created by Yuan's pen is one in which ghosts and spirits interact regularly with the corporeal world, sometimes in good humor and at other times with vengeful ferocity. An important part of these interactions is the certainty that inhumane treatment and hypocrisy will not be tolerated by the world of the dead.

One of the prominent themes in the collection is the injustice of the judicial system when controlled by heartless moralists or hypocrites. Tales such as "The Magistrate of Pinyang," "Quan Gu," and "The Female Impersonator" reveal the popular loathing of officials who impose harsh punishments on those accused of "sex crimes" such as premarital sex, adultery, or prostitution. In some of these tales the magistrate in question is depicted as deriving a vicarious, sadistic sexual pleasure in overseeing the punishment and humiliation of women. Punishments such as the beating of bared buttocks, the parading of tiny shoes, and the raping of women with cudgels are all inflicted in the name of "justice" and "morality." In Yuan's tales, however, these official sentences emerge ultimately as unjust, inhumane, and completely immoral—little more than a conservative charade. These accounts of hypocritical, moralistic administrators often end with the victim's ghost extracting revenge. Through these tales of the miscarriage of justice by excessively moralistic magistrates, Yuan vigorously opposes the state's right to interfere in what are essentially personal matters of private individuals. The magistrates, more often than not, are exposed as callously using the private affairs of others to buttress weak personal claims to superior moral standards.

Yuan's depiction of sexual pleasure is similarly challenging because it inherently rejects the need to pass moral judgment on people's sexual activities. While it has been argued that Yuan's morality was limited by his historical situation and that his tales are bound by the patriarchal attitudes of his times,[12] a casual reading of his stories shows that he clearly regards love and sexual pleasure as parts of the human condition that should be celebrated rather than denied or restricted. "The Cool Old Man" reflects this sentiment well in its depiction of an abbot, indeed a reincarnation of Buddha, reveling in the pleasures of sex. The diversity of sexual practice in Qing China, and its acceptance by the public, is another recurring theme in Yuan's *biji xiaoshuo.* "Double Blossom Temple" illustrates this point well. A temple has been built by local villagers to honor a homosexual couple brutally murdered by the local ruffian. After many years a passing official orders the temple razed because he cannot countenance a monument to such an "immoral practice" as homosexuality. The ghosts of the murdered couple then appear to the official in a dream and challenge the purity of his motives. How could an upright official be familiar with what went on between their sheets? they ask. The official's death is then predicted and the story ends with his execution.

Not all of the tales are as serious as these. Sexuality provides Yuan Mei with ample opportunity to exercise his lively sense of humor. Take, for example, "Little Mischief," in which a cheeky serving boy is seduced by the ghost of a young girl. He is so frightened when he discovers his lover is actually a ghost that he runs outside shrieking in alarm. Only after the entire household, women and men alike, come running to his aid does he realize he is stark naked. Similarly, in "Scholar Zhang" a timid scholar alone in his employer's garden late one night is nearly raped by a woman whom he assumes to be a ghost. She fails to accomplish the deed because the scholar has collapsed in terror and is unable to maintain an erection, despite all her efforts to arouse him. Describing him and his member as "absolutely useless," she storms off in disgust. The humorous public humiliation of the sexual inadequacies of Scholar Zhang and the youngster in "Little Mischief" reveal Yuan's enthusiasm for life and all its multifarious idiocies.

A belief in ghosts and their social hierarchy in the underworld is an important part of the Qing social order. To a certain extent Yuan Mei's ghost stories serve to empower the weak and vulnerable in society. Ghostly revenge against injustice is better than no revenge at all. Similarly, careful manipulation of the underworld by the living can generate tangible benefits for vulnerable people. See, for example, "A Ghost Buys Herself a Son," in which a new wife asserts her dominance and control over the household and ensures a rightful place for her son as the progeny of the deceased first wife by claiming to be possessed by the spirit of the latter. Each day the first wife's ghost enters the body of the new wife and takes control of the household's affairs. In short, the authority the new wife lacks is supplemented by her assumption of the deceased wife's spirit. A similar worldly manipulation of the general popular belief in ghosts occurs in "The Wooden Guardsmen." In this tale a number of young coppersmiths are sodomized each night in their sleep for more than a month. The search for the culprit begins and eventually the statue of a sentry guarding a temple is blamed. One of the victims recognizes the rapist's face, and the statue then has its feet nailed to the ground to prevent further assaults. Perhaps this was a convenient way for a human culprit to avoid discovery of what was rapidly becoming a highly risky nighttime pursuit.

Less contentious features of *Censored by Confucius* include the narration of strange natural phenomena. These are significant for their revelations about how seventeenth-century Chinese conceptualized themselves in the world. People who turn into animals, girls who turn into boys, huge windstorms, travels to strange lands, and shipwrecks are all featured in this collection. These tales ponder the mysteries of the natural world and the lands beyond China's borders.

Finally, the ghosts that fill this volume require explanation. The ghosts, demons, raccoons, and fox fairies of Yuan Mei's world are immensely human creatures filled with the full range of human quirks, virtues, and foibles. The bureaucrats of the underworld are just as likely to commit miscarriages of justice as their worldly counterparts. Take "The City God Gets Drunk" and "Swindled by the Earth God's Wife," in which gods invested with power and responsibility mismanage their affairs. Yuan's ghosts are no less likely to tolerate humiliation and injustice from moralistic meddlers than are his human characters. Human beings who fail to show appropriate respect for the dead often face the full force of the powers of the underworld. One such tale is

"Revenge of the Skull," in which a young man humiliates a skull by defecating in it. He is then chased by the skull and then dies a degrading death eating his own feces. "The Good Little Ghost" similarly sees the revenge of a ghost who can be described, in 1990s terms, as a victim of sexual harassment. The ghost seeks her revenge but unfortunately follows the wrong man home and drives an innocent man to his death. In sum, the world created by Yuan Mei in this contentious collection is lively, vengeful, funny, and frightening—and sometimes all of these at once.

We have chosen a representative selection of 100 tales from the full complement of 747 (excluding the sequel) with the intention of providing the reader with a taste of the richness of the *biji* genre as created by the genius of Yuan Mei.[13] This selection is intended to reveal the variation in themes, length, and narrative position possible within such brief jottings. Yet underlying these variations there remains the clear image of Yuan Mei as a man who was not to be drawn into petty moralism and who was a strong advocate of the right of each individual to self-determination.

## Notes

1. Yuan subsequently adopted the title *Xin Qi xie* (New wonder tales from Qi) for the collection when he discovered that a Yuan dynasty volume of stories titled *Zi bu yu* (Censored by Confucius) already existed. Yuan's collection, however, is still commonly known by its original title, *Zi bu yu.* (Wang Li et al. 1989, pp. 654–55).
2. Nivison comments on this invective, "Chang is probably as famous in China for his criticism of Yuan Mei as for anything he has written" (Nivison 1966, p. 264).
3. This beautiful property still exists and is a popular tourist spot.
4. For a discussion of the debate between Yuan and Zhang Xuecheng see Mann 1994.
5. One famous funeral inscription is "Ji mei wen" (Funeral ode to my younger sister), in Zhu et al. 1987, pp. 1557–64.
6. In recent years some Chinese critics have claimed that Western modernism leans heavily on *zhiguai* writing (see Yu 1992).
7. The translation of this book by Cheng et al. 1985 contains reproductions of the wonderful illustrations to be found in the original.
8. For more detailed history of the *biji* genre, see Liu 1987.
9. Zeitlin (1993) provides an excellent discussion of Pu Songling.
10. A few tales from Yuan's *Zi bu yu* have been translated, but there has been no book-length translation. See Waley 1956, pp. 120–31 (six tales); Ebrey 1981, pp. 181–84 (six tales); Chan 1991, pp. 40–47 (ten tales from the first volume and its sequel); Lo 1992, pp. 78–85 (nine tales from the first volume and its sequel).
11. For a selection of Ji Yun's *biji,* see Meng Zhaojin and Ma Peixin's edition of Ji's *Yuewei caotang biji* (Meng and Ma 1983). For a discussion of Ji's craft, see Keenan 1987.

12. Wang Yijia, a Taiwanese scholar, has analyzed *Zi bu yu* from a feminist perspective (1989, pp. 213–28).

13. The edition we have used for this translation is the 1788 edition reprinted by Taipei's Xingguang chubanshe in 1989.

## Bibliography

Birch, Cyril, ed. 1972. *Anthology of Chinese Literature.* New York: Grove Weidenfeld.

Chan, Leo Tak-hung. 1991. "Subjugating Spirits: Yuan Mei's *What the Master Would Not Speak Of.*" *Asian Culture* 19, no. 4: 40–47.

Cheng Hsiao-Chieh et al., trans. 1985. *Shan Hai Ching: Legendary Geography and Wonders in Ancient China.* Taipei: National Institute for Compilation and Translation.

Ebrey, Patricia. 1981. *Chinese Civilization and Society: A Sourcebook.* New York: Free Press.

Giles, Herbert, trans. 1880. *Strange Stories from a Chinese Studio.* Rpt. 1916. Shanghai: Kelly & Walsh.

Keenan, David L. 1987. "The Forms and Uses of the Ghost Story in Late Eighteenth Century China as Recorded in the *Yueh wei ts'ao t'ang pi-chi* of Chi Yün." Ph.D. dissertation, Harvard University.

Lau, D. C., trans. 1979. *Confucius: The Analects.* Rpt. 1982. Harmondsworth, England: Penguin.

Legge, James, trans. 1893. *Confucian Analects.* In *The Chinese Classics,* vol. 1. Rpt. 1985. Taipei: Southern Materials Centre.

Liu Yeqiu. 1987. *Lidai biji gaishu* (An outline history of *biji* writing). Taipei: Muduo chubanshe.

Lo, Irving Yucheng, and William Shultz. 1986. *Waiting for the Unicorn: Poems and Lyrics Of China's Last Dynasty 1644–1911.* Bloomington: Indiana University Press.

Lo Yuet Keung. 1992. "New Wonder Tales of Qi: Excerpts." *Renditions* (Spring): 78–85.

Ma, Y. M. 1986. "Pi-chi." Pp. 650–52 in *Indiana Companion to Classical Chinese Literature,* ed. W. H. Nienhauser. Bloomington: Indiana University Press.

Mann, Susan. 1994. "Learned Women in the Eighteenth Century." Pp. 27–46 in *Engendering China: Women, Culture and the State,* ed. C. K. Gilmartin et al. Cambridge: Harvard University Press.

Meng Zhaojin and Ma Peixin, eds. 1983. *"Yuewei caotang biji" gushi xuan* (Jottings of close observations from the thatched abode). Shijiazhuang: Huashan wenyi chubanshe.

Nivison, David S. 1966. *The Life and Thought of Chang Hsüeh-ch'eng (1738–1801).* Stanford, Ca.: Stanford University Press.

Shen Meng. 1988. "Qianyan" (Preface). In *Zi bu yu xuanzhu* (A selected annotation of *Zi bu yu*). Beijing: Wenhua yishu chubanshe.

Spence, Jonathan. 1977. "Ch'ing." Pp. 259–94 in *Food in Chinese Culture,* ed. K. C. Chang. New Haven: Yale University Press.

Waley, Arthur. 1956. *Yuan Mei: Eighteenth Century Chinese Poet.* London: George Allen & Unwin.

Wang Li et al., eds. 1989. *Zhongguo gudai wenxue cidian* (Classical Chinese literature dictionary). Nanning: Guangxi jiaoyu chubanshe.

Wang Yijia. 1989. *Gudian jinkan: Cong Kong Ming dao Pan Jinlian* (The classics from a modern perspective: From Kong Ming to Pan Jinlian). Taipei: Ye'e chubanshe.

Yang Tao. 1992. *Yuan Zicai waizhuan* (The unofficial biography of Yuan Mei). Taipei: Shijie wenwu chubanshe.

Yu Rujie. 1992. *Xian gui yao ren: Zhiguai chuanqi xinlun* (Immortals, ghosts, monsters, and people: A new theory of *zhiguai* and *chuanqi*). Beijing: Zhongguo gongren chubanshe.

Yuan Mei. 1972. "Seven Poems on Aging," trans. Arthur Waley. Pp. 197–200 in *Anthology of Chinese Literature*, ed. Cyril Birch. New York: Grove Weidenfeld.

———. 1788. *Zi bu yu*. Rpt. 1989. Taipei: Xingguang chubanshe.

Zeitlin, Judith. 1993. *Historian of the Strange: Pu Songling and the Chinese Classical Tale*. Stanford, Ca.: Stanford University Press.

Zhu Dongren et al., eds. 1987. *Guwen jianshang cidian* (Companion to classical literary appreciation). Nanjing: Jiangsu wenyi chubanshe.

# CENSORED BY CONFUCIUS

# *Deputy Prefect Li*

The deputy prefect of Guangxi Province was an extremely wealthy man by the name of Li. He kept seven concubines and owned many priceless treasures and jewels. Tragically, this wealthy young sub-prefect was only twenty-seven when he fell ill and died.

Among the numerous members of his household was an elderly servant of impeccable honesty and unfailing loyalty. Of course, he sorely grieved the loss of his beloved young master. He and the concubines built a little shrine in Li's honor and this became the focus of their ritual prayers and fasting.

One day a wandering Daoist monk came knocking at the door to beg for alms.

The elderly servant scolded him, saying, "Our young master has just passed away, and here you are asking us for alms!"

The Daoist laughed. "So, you wish he were back here among you, do you? Well, then, I can do a little magic for you and bring him back if you like," he said mysteriously.

The old servant was overjoyed at this news and rushed inside to tell the concubines. The women were all very surprised to learn that such a miracle was possible and they hurried out to meet the Daoist. He had vanished, however.

This sorely missed opportunity generated no small amount of rancor among the women gathered at the gate. Each one blamed the next for offending a Daoist immortal and they returned to their quarters, all rather disgruntled.

Not long after this first meeting, the elderly servant saw the Daoist at the local market performing various religious rites. Greatly excited by this chance meeting, he rushed over to beg forgiveness for his earlier rudeness.

In response to the servant's request for help the Daoist said, "I didn't leave because I didn't want to help return your master. It was just that there's a regulation in the underworld that a replacement life must be given up for the one to be reborn. I assumed that there was nobody in your household who would want to take the young master's place in the world of the dead, so I just wandered off again."

The old servant then asked deferentially, "I would be very grateful if you would come back with me so we can discuss the problem with the young mistresses." After much coaxing the Daoist was persuaded to return to the house.

The elderly man went inside first to explain to the concubines. Of course, the women were delighted to hear that the Daoist had been found. But on learning that someone would have to die for their husband, they instantly fell into a resentful silence, each one looking expectantly at the next.

The elderly servant then said determinedly, "You are all so young that if any of you were to die it would be a great shame. As for me, though, I am so old and decrepit that I might as well be dead."

He returned to the waiting Daoist. "Would it be all right if I replaced my master?"

The Daoist replied, "It should be all right as long as you have no regrets and show no fear."

"I'll do it," the servant said decisively.

"Well, then," said the Daoist, "since you have resolved to do this, you should go and make your farewells to all your friends and relatives. I'll stay here and prepare the magic. It should be ready in three days, and by the end of the week we should have the results."

The elderly servant then arranged rooms for the Daoist, and over the next few days he ensured that the priest was served with the respect due a distinguished visitor. In between, he rushed around town bidding farewell to friends and relatives.

Their reactions to his strange news were mixed. Some laughed at his stupidity, others respected his loyalty, while others pitied him. Of course there were also many who simply did not believe that he was really going to go through with such a crazy scheme.

During one of these expeditions the elderly man passed by the temple of Guandi, the god of war. As he had always been a believer in this particular god, he went in to pray for guidance in preparing for his impending sacrificial death.

He chanted: "I beseech you, oh Guandi, to assist the Daoist in returning my master's soul to his hearth and home."

He had just finished his prayer when a barefoot monk standing at the base of the altar shouted at him: "You have the aura of an evil spirit hanging over you! Disaster lies ahead! But if you keep our meeting a secret, I can save you from this fate."

He then gave the servant a small packet. "When the time comes, open this packet and you will be saved." In an instant the monk was gone.

When the elderly servant returned home, he carefully opened the packet and found wrapped inside a set of five fingernails and a piece of rope. Puzzled, he rewrapped the package and placed it carefully in his pocket.

When the three days of preparation came to an end, the Daoist told the servant to bring his bed into the room where the young master's coffin was housed, and to place it across from the coffin. He then put locks on all the doors and windows and cut a hole in the wall to allow food to be passed in to the servant to sustain him while he waited for the magic to take effect. Finally, the Daoist erected an altar near the concubines' quarters.

Nothing happened for two days and the elderly servant began to doubt that anything would. Then suddenly he heard wind gusting up from under the bed.

Two dark figures about two feet high emerged from the floorboards. Their greenish eyes were set deep in heads the size of wagon wheels and their bodies were covered with short bristles. They stared at the elderly servant, then slowly made their way to the coffin, where they set about gnashing a hole in it.

As the hole grew larger the servant could hear coughing from inside. It sounded just like the young master! Then, the two demons opened the lid of the coffin and helped the young master out. He was clearly very weak and sick, but the demons began to massage his abdomen and eventually sound issued from his lips.

The elderly servant looked carefully at the person before him and it soon became clear that while the body was that of the young master, the voice belonged to the Daoist. He came to the grim realization that the words he had heard in Guandi's temple were true, so he quickly drew the package from his chest pocket and carefully opened it.

The five fingernails flew off in the form of a golden dragon dozens of feet long. The dragon picked the elderly servant up and flew through the air with him, bringing him to rest on the roof beams, where he found himself bound with ropes.

Though semi-conscious by now, the servant could see the demons helping the newly revived master to his now empty bed. Suddenly the master shouted in anguish, "My magic is failing!"

At this the two demons became quite vicious and angrily searched the room for the elderly man. The master grew violent, shredding the servant's bedding and all his bed curtains. By chance, one of the demons looked up and saw the servant tied to the roof beam. Jubilant the master jumped up, trying to pull him down.

Just then there was a tremendous crack of thunder. The elderly man fell to the floor, the coffin closed up, and the demons sunk through the floorboards as quickly as they had emerged.

On hearing the crack of thunder, the concubines rushed in to see what had happened. The elderly servant told them every detail of his ordeal, and when the women learned about the Daoist's treachery they hurried to see what had become of him. On the altar lay the corpse of the Daoist—he had been struck by lightning—and etched upon his body in a sulfureous dust was his story.

It was written that the evil Daoist had been using his magical powers to gain access to money and sex by using other people's bodies. Heaven had decreed that he be executed for his crimes, and so it was done.

# *Scholar Cai*

Outside the north gate of Hangzhou's city wall was a house that was reputed to be haunted. As a consequence, nobody dared live there and so the house remained vacant and firmly sealed.

One day a scholar by the name of Cai came by and expressed his wish to purchase the house. The locals tried to dissuade him, saying he would be risking his life if he tried to live in such a place. But Cai paid them no heed and proceeded with the purchase, signing all the necessary documents. His family refused to take up residence, however, so Cai moved in by himself.

On his first night in the house he sat up with a candle to keep watch. At midnight a woman with a red sash dangling from her neck quietly entered his room. She curtsied and the two exchanged greetings. Then the woman tied a rope to the roof beam and pulled the noose over her head. Throughout this performance Cai remained unruffled. Next, she tied another rope and beckoned to Cai to join her. Cai accepted her invitation but drew the noose over his foot.

The woman said, "My dear sir, that's the wrong way."

Cai laughed. "I'm certainly not wrong. You're the one who's doing it the wrong way and that's why you ended up where you are today."

At this, the ghost fell to her knees weeping, and after bowing to Cai several times she left. From this time on, the house was free of supernatural occurrences. Cai, moreover, was successful in his examinations. Some say he may be the local magistrate, Cai Binghou.

## *Revenge of the Skull*

Sun Junshou of Changshu was extremely cruel and vicious and took particular delight in mocking ghosts and spirits. One day, while he and some friends were up in the hills having a picnic, Sun found himself in need of a place to empty his bowels. Looking around for a suitable spot he came across a dilapidated grave where a skull lay exposed on the ground. Sun squatted over the upturned skull and defecated into the opening, saying, "How did you enjoy that, my good fellow?"

Much to Sun's horror, the skull opened its mouth and replied, "Exquisite!"

Terrified, Sun ran as fast as his feet could carry him. But the skull rolled along like a wheel behind, and it was only when Sun had crossed a bridge that the skull ceased its pursuit. Climbing a hill on the other side of the bridge, Sun glanced back to see the skull rolling back to the grave.

By the time Sun reached home his face was a deathly gray and he had become incontinent. Until his death three days later the man would eat his own feces and ask himself, "How did you enjoy that, my good fellow?" And then he would defecate and eat his feces all over again.

# *General Zhao Spears the Cheeky Monster*

After waging campaigns against rebels in the mountainous borderlands General Zhao Liangdong passed through Chengdu in Sichuan Province. He was welcomed on his arrival by the governor of Sichuan and escorted to the house of a local citizen to spend the night.

When he arrived at the house General Zhao discovered that the rooms he had been allocated were extremely cramped, so he asked to stay in the yamen of the western district.

In reply the governor explained, "I would have had the yamen prepared for your arrival but I'm told it is haunted. It's been locked up for over a century now."

General Zhao smiled. "Over the course of my life I've defeated hordes of bandits, quelled many rebellions, and slaughtered countless numbers of men. If those ghosts and demons know what's good for them they'll stay out of my way!"

He promptly gave the order for the yamen to be cleaned out in preparation for his personal use. The general housed his family in the inner quarters while he himself took a bed in the main room. As he lay down to sleep he put his long military lance under his pillow.

At the second watch, the hooks of the bed curtains clanged together and there in front of the bed stood a tall white-gowned figure with a bulbous belly. In the shadow of the lamplight its face had a cold and greenish glow.

General Zhao sat up and shouted fiercely at the ghost, who promptly took several steps back into the circle of lamplight. The momentary illumination of his face showed the gruesome visage of a guardian god from a folk painting. Zhao thrust out with his lance but the ghost dodged behind a wall support. Zhao thrust out his lance again, and once more the ghost dodged. It then slipped quickly into a small crack in the wall and disappeared.

As General Zhao walked back to his room he sensed he was being followed. He swung around and found the ghost sneaking up behind him with a broad grin on its face.

The general was furious at such insolence. "How is it that such a cheeky monster is allowed to exist?!"

Woken by the commotion, Zhao's servants rushed for their weapons and advanced on the ghost *en masse*. The ghost beat a hasty retreat into an empty room through a crack in the wall. Clouds of dust and sand rose up and the waiting servants expected, from the volume of noise, to see a horde of ugly reinforcements. Instead the ghost made its way through to the main hall again. He stood up tall and then crouched over, assuming a fighting position.

The servants were terrified at this change of tactics and nobody dared to advance on the ghost. The general, however, had grown increasingly angry and he took up his own lance and speared the monster through the belly. As the lance pierced the bulge, a strange sound could be heard and then the ghost's body disappeared.

Eventually, all that remained was the dazzling metallic gleam of two golden eyes the size of large copper basins, hanging from the wall. The servants struck out at the eyes with their swords and these dazzling lights soon transformed into sparks and stars that lit up the entire room. Gradually these too diminished.

Then dawn arrived.

Before he mounted his horse to take his leave of Chengdu, General Zhao told all the city officials about the night's strange events. They all gaped in amazement. Nobody was ever able to determine the exact nature of this particular monster.

# *The Magistrate of Pingyang*

The magistrate of Pingyang, a man by the name of Zhu Shuo, was renowned for the extremely cruel way he meted out punishments. Indeed, the cangues and cudgels produced in the territories under his jurisdiction were particularly thick and heavy.

In all cases involving women, Magistrate Zhu would be sure to give a moralizing lecture on adultery. His punishment of prostitutes involved stripping them and repeatedly ramming cudgels up their vaginas, ensuring that they remained swollen for several months. The magistrate would then declare, "Let's see her take a client now!" and promptly order that clients' faces be smeared with blood from the prostitutes' buttocks.

If the prostitutes were beautiful he would be even more brutal, saying, "If all beautiful women are made to be plain, then our society will be rid of the scourge of prostitution!" He would then order the prostitutes' heads shaved and their nostrils slashed.

He often bragged of this to his colleagues: "I am totally impervious to sexual desire. How would I be able to mete out such punishments if I didn't have a heart of stone?"

When Zhu had completed his term in Pingyang he was reassigned to Shandong. During the shift, he and his family stayed in a guesthouse in Chiping County. The top floor of the guesthouse was firmly sealed and when Zhu asked the innkeeper why, he was told, "There are ghosts up there so the floor has been kept locked for many years."

Zhu replied in his typically obstinate manner, "What possible reason do we have to be scared? When those specters hear of my reputation, I guarantee they'll beat a hasty retreat."

Despite his wife's desperate entreaties he rented the upper floor, put his family in one room, and, armed with a sword, kept watch by candlelight in another.

At the third drum there was a knock at his door and a white-haired man wearing a dark red cap entered. When he saw Zhu the old man bowed reverently, but in reply Zhu simply shouted at him, demanding that the specter identify himself.

The old man replied: "I am not a specter. I am the local earth god and it is with great pleasure that I welcome you here tonight. When I heard of your arrival I knew that the time for the exorcism of the ghosts dwelling here was nigh."

He then went on to say, "In a little while the ghosts will appear. If we are to take all their heads you should first strike them with your sword and then I'll be able to come in and help you."

Zhu was immensely pleased by this news and thanked the old man before bidding him farewell.

Presently a green-faced demon and a white-faced demon did indeed appear before Zhu. Zhu struck out with his sword, slicing one and then the other. Then some long-toothed, black-mouthed demons appeared and Zhu again struck out with his sword. The demons screamed in pain and fell to the ground. Zhu was extremely proud of his performance and hurried down to tell the innkeeper about the night's events.

By this time the rooster had crowed and the other residents had risen, so they all went up with their candles to survey the scene. Under the flickering candlelight they saw the floor strewn with the corpses of Zhu's wife, concubines, and children.

Zhu screamed, "I've been tricked by the ghosts and specters!" Then, grief-stricken, he collapsed to the floor, dead.

# *Tricking the Thunder God*

Zhao Licun, a demobilized soldier from Nanfeng County, once told me of a strange event that occurred during the Ming dynasty. The story had been passed down from one of his ancestors, a man of exceptional talent who lived in the village in question.

At one point, when the anarchy and chaos of the Ming had reached its peak, the village was repeatedly terrorized by bandits who would extort money from the locals during festivals and the like. It wasn't long before the villagers' suffering became intolerable, so Zhao took it upon himself to report these criminals to the law. The bandits were forthwith officially banned from entering the village and this left them without their primary source of income. Naturally, they were furious.

Because Zhao had official backing, the bandits couldn't personally take revenge on him, so they decided to invoke a higher authority. Whenever thunder clouds banked up on the horizon, the bandits would gather together with all their wives and children and pray to the thunder god for assistance, chanting: "Please strike down that evil Mr. Zhao."

Their prayers were accompanied by ritual sacrifices of pigs and the like, and were not without results.

One day, Mr. Zhao was pottering around in his garden when suddenly there was a great crashing boom. A sulfureous smell filled the garden and down from the sky came a hairy fellow with a mouth like a beak. Zhao recognized this to be the thunder god and deduced that he must have been tricked by the bandits.

He quickly threw the nearby chamber pot at the thunder god, shouting: "Thunder god! In all the fifty years I've been alive, I've never seen you dare to strike a tiger! You always pick on the humble water buffalo! What is it that makes you victimize the weak and gentle? How can you be such a bully? What's your purpose in coming here? Go on, then, you can destroy me or simply ruin me, but you know, I won't hate you, I'll just pity you!"

The thunder god, soaked in urine from the chamber pot, was rendered speechless by this tirade. Behind his angry eyes was the glimmer of shame. He fell in a heap to the ground and began what turned out to be three days of pitiful crying.

When the bandits heard of this strange turn of events they were greatly moved and admitted, "It was our request that brought this hardship and embarrassment to the thunder god." They called upon a Daoist monk and asked him to help the thunder god with prayers. This was carried out and the thunder god left.

*Thunder God*

## *Ghosts Are Afraid of Those Unafraid of Death*

One of Official Jie's cousins was an exceptionally strong and fearless sort. He particularly loathed people spreading frightening tales about ghosts, and always chose to live in places reputed to be haunted.

One day, while traveling through Shandong Province, he stopped at an inn that was rumored to have some sort of demon living in its western wing. Jie, extremely pleased to be presented with such a challenge, immediately arranged to rent the rooms for the night.

At the second watch a tile was knocked from the roof.

In reply Jie cursed loudly. "If you're really a decent ghost then you'd throw something down that can't be found on a roof. Perhaps then I'd be afraid of you."

Surely enough a grinding stone was tossed down. Jie shouted back, "If you're really a fierce ghost I dare you to come and destroy my table. Then maybe I'd be scared of you."

Surely enough a huge stone came hurtling through the air and smashed half of his table.

Jie was furious and screamed, "You damned mongrel of a ghost! I'll bow to you only when you've smashed my head in!"

He promptly stood up, threw his hat to the floor, lifted his head, and waited for the assault.

After this stand-off no more strange sounds could be heard and thenceforth all supernatural happenings in this wing of the building ceased.

# *Scholar Qiu*

One summer's day a Nanchang scholar by the name of Qiu took a nap in the cool of the local earth god's temple. After returning home he became extremely ill. Qiu's wife decided that he must have offended the earth god, and she prepared offerings and burnt incense to placate the spirit. Surely enough, Qiu then regained his health.

His wife advised him to return to the temple to show his gratitude to the god. But Qiu was furious and instead filed a letter of complaint against the earth god, accusing him of using his powers to squeeze food and wine from the people. He sent this complaint to the city god by burning the letter. However, after ten days nothing had happened.

Qiu became even more furious and burned a second letter of complaint. This letter included an additional reference to the city god's own behavior, suggesting that by being lax with corrupt subordinates he was himself undeserving of any offerings.

That night he dreamed that a notice had been posted on the wall of the city god's temple. It read: "The local earth god is extorting food and drink from the people and has thereby abused his office. He is setting a bad example and as a consequence should lose his position. This man Qiu does not respect ghosts and spirits and pokes his nose into the affairs of others. He should be sent to Xinjian and be given twenty strokes."

After waking, Qiu remained convinced that the dream signified nothing. After all, he was a Nanchang resident, so even if he were to be punished, it would not be in Xinjian.

Not long after, there was a huge storm during which the earth god's temple was struck by lightning. Qiu became a bit worried and decided it would be safer to stay inside for a while. After a few weeks had passed without event he relaxed his guard.

One day, not long after this, the inspector of Jiangxi came to a nearby temple to pray. While praying he happened to be struck on the forehead by an axe. This event caused great consternation among the local officials, and they assembled at the scene to determine who should take responsibility. Scholar Qiu got wind of the spectacle and hurried over to watch.

One of the officials, the magistrate of Xinjian, thought Qiu's behavior rather odd. Suspecting him of being the culprit, he demanded that Qiu identify himself. Poor Qiu was terrified and could only stammer incoherently. From the clothing Qiu wore, the magistrate deduced that he was unlikely to be anyone of consequence, and in a fit of fury at Qiu's insolence he ordered that Qiu receive twenty strokes.

It was only after these strokes had been administered that Qiu regained his power of speech. "I am Scholar Qiu of the Qiu Sinong household," he said.

Hearing that his criminal was actually a scholar, the magistrate regretted his hasty verdict. To compensate Qiu for his suffering, the magistrate employed him as head teacher at Fengcheng.

*City God and Earth God*

# *Ghosts Have Only Three Tricks*

Mr. Cai Wei was often heard to say, "Ghosts have three tricks. Initially they will attempt to enchant. Failing that, they will venture to block, and finally they will resort to terrorizing."

When asked to expound upon his theory he would reply, "I have a cousin by the name of Lü who is a scholarship student at Songjiang. He has a very open and direct personality, and indeed his self-styled nickname is Mr. Direct.

"One evening he passed through a village west of Lake Liu. Dusk had just fallen when he saw a woman, her face powdered and rouged, hurrying along with a rope in her hands. When she saw Lü, she tried to avoid him by hastening to the shelter of a large tree. In doing so she dropped her rope. Lü picked it up. It proved to be a straw rope exuding the sweet, sickly smell of blood. He quickly concluded that the woman was a ghost and had died from hanging. He hid the rope under his clothing and walked on ahead.

"The woman came out from behind the tree and tried to block Lü's path. When he walked to the left she would move to the left; when he walked to the right she would move to the right. Lü recognized this ploy as 'playing the ghostly wall.' So, he rushed directly towards her. The ghost was caught unawares, but then with one long shrill cry she transformed herself into a blood-soaked figure covered by long hair. She poked out her tongue and skipped towards Lü.

"Lü said, 'At first you tried to enchant me with your rouge and powder. Then you ventured to block my path. Now you have adopted this gruesome form in an attempt to scare me. Your three tricks are used up, and I am still not scared. I know you have no other ploys. Didn't you realize that my name was Mr. Direct?'

"The ghost then resumed her original form and knelt on the ground before Lü, confessing, 'I am a city woman by the name of Shi. In a fit of anger after an argument with my husband I hanged myself. I have just heard that to the east of Lake Liu there lives a woman who is also having marital problems. I was hurrying there in the hope of finding a replacement ghost. I was not expecting you, sir, to impede my progress by taking my rope. It is true that I have no more tricks left, so I beg you to have mercy. Help me escape the horrors of hell. Help me be reincarnated.'

"Lü thereupon inquired, 'How can you achieve reincarnation?'

"To this she replied, 'If you ask my family, the Shis who live in the city, to hire priests and monks to chant prayers, or arrange for a high priest to chant the Reincarnation Sutra for me, I will be reincarnated.'

"Lü laughed and said, 'I am a high priest and moreover I am familiar with the Reincarnation Sutra. I will recite it for you.' And he sang aloud, 'This is a wonderful world. It has no obstacles and no hindrances. Life and death are one so why talk about replacements? When it is time to go, why not go? It is much simpler that way!'

"The instant she heard these words the ghost achieved enlightenment. She prostrated herself before Lü and then made a hasty departure."

According to the local people, that particular area had long been haunted, but no more supernatural events occurred there after Mr. Direct passed through.

# *Master Chen Qingke Blows the Ghost Away*

Before Master Chen became an official, he was friendly with an impoverished scholar from his native district by the name of Li Fu. One autumn evening while the moon was bright, Chen wandered over to Li's residence to pass some time.

Li was rather embarrassed and said to Chen, "My wife tells me there is nothing to drink in the house, so please have a seat while I go out and buy some wine. We'll be able to appreciate the moon more fully if we drink some wine."

Chen took out a volume of poetry to read while he waited for his friend to return.

A moment later the gate was pushed open and a woman with matted hair and tattered clothing came into the courtyard. As soon as she saw Chen she made as if to leave. Chen, assuming the woman was a relative of Li's who was embarrassed by the presence of a guest, turned his back, enabling her to slip inside unhindered.

Before the woman entered the house, she drew something from her sleeve and slipped it under the doorstep. Chen was puzzled by this behavior, and as soon as she had gone inside he went to find out what she had hidden.

Beneath the step he found a length of rope that exuded the sickly sweet stench of stale blood. He quickly concluded that she must be the ghost of a woman who had hanged herself. After hiding the rope in his shoe he sat down again.

After a while the woman with matted hair reappeared. She slipped her hand under the doorstep intending to retrieve her rope. When she found it was gone she was incensed. Rushing at Chen she screamed, "Give me back my things!"

Chen replied, "What things?"

Instead of answering, the woman stood stock still, opened her mouth, and blew towards Chen. Her breath was so cold that his hair stood on end and he broke into uncontrollable shivering. The flame of his candle flickered with a bluish light and was almost extinguished.

Then Chen thought to himself, "Ghosts aren't the only ones who have breath. I have it too!"

He inhaled deeply and blew hard towards the woman. Wherever his breath touched her form, a cavity appeared. At first there was a cavity in her abdomen, then there was a hole in her chest, and then her head vanished. Soon she had disappeared entirely, blown away like thin smoke.

Shortly after this, Li, carrying the wine, came running in shouting that his wife had been throttled in her bed.

Chen laughed. "Don't worry, the ghost's rope is here in my shoe." As they went inside to tend to Li's wife, Chen told Li of the strange events just past.

They managed to revive Li's wife by forcing some ginger broth down her throat. As soon as she was able to talk they questioned her about her attempted suicide.

She explained, "Although we are extremely poor, you insist on spending money to entertain your friends. Tonight you took my last remaining hair clasp to pawn for Chen's wine, and even though I was deeply distressed, I couldn't make a scene because Chen was just outside.

"All of a sudden, a woman with matted hair appeared beside me and introduced herself as our neighbor to the left. She told me that you had pawned the clasp to go gambling and were not intending to entertain Master Chen at all. Hearing this I became even more distressed and angry. It grew later and later and still you hadn't returned with the wine. What's more, Master Chen was still waiting outside and I didn't have the nerve to ask him to leave.

"Then the woman with matted hair made a circle with her hands and said, 'If you enter this circle then you will reach a Buddhist paradise of limitless joy.' But when I stepped up to her circle, she put her hands around my throat and squeezed as tightly as she could. Her grip, however, wasn't tight enough and the circle kept loosening.

"Then the woman said, 'I'll have to fetch my Buddha ribbon to help you achieve nirvana.' She went outside to get this ribbon but she never returned. From then on until you revived me, I drifted in and out of consciousness—it was all like a dream."

When the three made inquiries in the neighborhood, they discovered that a village woman had indeed hanged herself several months earlier.

# *The Tall Ghost Is Captured*

When the Hanlin academician Shen Houyu of Zhudun was young, he was the classmate of a friend of mine by the name of Zhang. Once, Zhang was absent from class for several days running. On inquiring, Shen discovered that Zhang had contracted a severe case of influenza.

Shen thereupon decided to pay Zhang a courtesy call. On arriving at the Zhang residence, Shen quietly went in through the front gate and was about to enter the main hall when he saw a tall, thin man reading the horizontal tablet in the hall.

Shen suspected that this was no less than an intruder. Playfully, he untied his belt, crept up to the intruder and quickly bound his legs.

With a look of complete surprise the tall man swung around to face Shen. Shen promptly interrogated him regarding the nature of his business and his place of origin.

The tall man explained, "Mr. Zhang is about to die. As a courier of death from the underworld, it is my duty to ensure that the matter is first cleared with the gods of his ancestral hall. Only after this formality is completed can his departure from this world be ensured."

Shen knew that Zhang's widowed mother was still alive and that Zhang himself was as yet unmarried and therefore without an heir, and so he entreated the tall man to find some way of helping Zhang escape death. The tall man was greatly moved but explained that there was nothing he could do.

Shen continued his sincere entreaties until eventually the tall man admitted, "There is one possible option. Zhang is due to die at noon tomorrow. Before that time, five guardians of death will be sent here with me. They will enter through the willow tree just outside. Now, because ghosts in the nether world have long been starved of food and drink, once they indulge themselves they often forget their purpose.

"Tomorrow you should prepare a banquet for six people and wait outside the house. When you feel a gust of wind blow past, that will signal their arrival. Greet them and welcome them inside to sit down and eat. At all times ensure that they are waited upon with the utmost respect. Only when the shadow of the sun signals the end of the day can you assume that the feasting is over. If you perform these deeds, then Zhang will be saved."

Shen agreed to organize the feast as requested and immediately went off to notify Zhang's family.

At the appointed time everything went according to the tall man's instructions. By morning Zhang had lost consciousness, and by noon he was on the point of death. Much to Shen's relief, however, Zhang's color returned when the banquet was completed.

One night a month later, Shen dreamed that the tall man was gazing at him with a furrowed brow and a face etched with pain.

The man said, "I devised a plan for you so that Mr. Zhang could live another dozen years. He will pass his examinations and become a candidate in the provincial college, as well as raise two sons. But as for me, I was punished with forty strokes and the loss of my job because somebody exposed my disclosure of the underworld's secrets. I am in fact not a ghost but a porter from Xiashi County by the name of Liu Xian.

"Since the beatings I can no longer walk. I am fated, however, to live for three more years. In my crippled state I have no way of making a living and I need you to ask Mr. Zhang to provide me with an allowance that would enable me to endure the rest of my days."

Shen relayed the message to Zhang, who immediately gathered a generous supply of gold, arranged the purchase of a boat, and went with Shen to visit the porter. Surely enough, they found the man paralyzed and bedridden. Bowing before the bed, they gave the man all the gold they had brought to show their gratitude for the risk he had taken.

Thereafter the events foretold in the dream regarding Mr. Zhang's success did indeed occur as predicted.

# *The Lady Ghost of the Western Garden*

A man by the name of Zhou who hailed from Hangzhou went traveling with his friend, a Mr. Chen. During their journey they stopped at the Han River and stayed with a local gentry family.

Although it was nearly autumn, the summer heat lingered, making the rooms they were given feel rather stuffy and cramped. There were, however, several tidy little houses in the western garden of the residence. These faced the hills and a lake and generally looked a lot cooler and quieter than their present rooms. So the two men moved their beds into one of the little houses and slept very well indeed.

One evening they decided to take a walk in the cool of the evening to admire the moon, and it was about the second watch by the time they returned. Before they had completed their preparations for sleep they heard footsteps in the courtyard and then the sound of someone slowly reciting a poem: "The spring flowers have gone, and the autumn moon is here. Glancing round I see distant Mount Wu, and the hair on my temple continues to gray."

At first they thought it might be their host taking a walk. But the voice was not at all like his and so they quickly put on their clothes and peered out into the moonlight. There before them was a beautiful woman, leaning gracefully against the fence. The two men whispered their surprise, for neither had heard mention of such a woman in the household. She wore clothes that were clearly not the contemporary fashion, so they deduced that she was either a ghost or a spirit.

Chen, a youthful sort who was easily aroused, said carelessly, "She's so incredibly beautiful I really couldn't care if she's a ghost or a demon!" He then called out, "Look here, my beauty! Come in and chat with us for a while!"

From outside the courtyard came the reply, "Why should I come in? Why don't you come out?"

Chen grabbed Zhou by the arm and rushed outside. Strangely

enough, there was nobody there. So they called out and then followed the direction of the reply. This continued for a while and soon the two men found themselves among trees.

Peering through the darkness, they suddenly saw a woman's head hanging from a willow tree. They screamed in horror only to see the head fall to the ground and bounce towards them. They rushed back to the courtyard with the head close on their heels, slammed the door shut, and pushed against it with all their might to prevent the head from breaking through. Undeterred, the head began to gnaw ferociously at the door, grinding and crunching.

Just when the men thought that the head was going to catch them, a rooster crowed, signaling the new day. Instantly the gnawing ceased and the head bounded back towards the lake and disappeared. As soon as it was well and truly light, Chen and Zhou moved their bedding back into their former cramped rooms. Both men were sick for more than ten days after this episode.

# *A Sentry Is Struck by Lightning*

In 1738, during the Qianlong emperor's reign, a sentry died after being struck by lightning. The event was considered rather strange by those who knew the dead man because he was generally thought of as a decent sort of fellow.

Then an old soldier told the deceased's story. "Although he has lived a decent life these last few years, twenty years ago, after he joined the forces, there was a nasty incident involving him that I got to hear about, since we were in the same platoon. The general had arranged to do some hunting in the Gaoting Mountain region and our now-dead colleague was instructed to set up camp along the road.

"It so happened that as night was falling a young nun came walking past the tents. The soldier, checking first that no one was around, dragged her into one of the tents and tried to rape her. She fought back and was finally able to escape, albeit without her trousers. The soldier chased the nun for quite some time, but when she took refuge in a farmhouse he had to return to the campsite unsatisfied.

"At the time, the mistress of the farmhouse was alone with her small son, since her husband, a casual laborer, was still out working. She was not at all keen to let this strange nun into her house, but after the nun explained what had happened and begged for assistance the woman softened and drew her inside. The nun borrowed a pair of trousers and promised to return them within three days. By dawn the next day the nun had left the house.

"When the laborer returned home for a fresh pair of clothes, his wife discovered that in her haste she must have given the nun her husband's trousers instead of her own, since there were no more clean trousers belonging to her husband in the chest. Annoyed by her mistake, she was just about to explain everything to her husband when their young boy said, 'A monk came last night and wore them home.'

"The husband grew suspicious and pressed the boy for more details.

The boy told him that the previous night a monk had come and asked his mother for shelter, taken the trousers, and left while it was still dark. The wife frantically explained that it was a nun, not a monk, but her husband was furious and beat her as punishment. When he checked his wife's story with the neighbors, he found that none of them had seen anything. His wife, for her part, couldn't bear the injustice of his accusations and so she hanged herself.

"The day after her death, the man answered a knock at his door to find a young nun, carrying the trousers and bearing a basket of pastries as thanks. The little boy pointed at the nun and said, 'That's the monk who came and stayed the other night.' The man was overcome with remorse at the gravity of his mistake. He dragged his son to the foot of the wife's coffin, beat the boy to death, then hanged himself. The neighbors, unwilling to face a huge official inquiry, simply buried the bodies and let the matter rest.

"The next winter, when the general returned to the same locality to hunt, someone mentioned the tragedy to him. I knew it was this sentry who had precipitated the unfortunate chain of events, but since the case had gone no further, I decided to let the matter rest. Later on, when we were alone, I told the sentry what had happened. Naturally, he was extremely worried. From then on he lived a life of virtue hoping to atone for his sins. Ultimately, however, heaven will exact its punishment."

# *In Which Hunters Expurgate the Fox Fairies*

In the town of Yuanhua in Haichang County there lived a wealthy family whose habit it was to work on the lower floor during the day, thus leaving the three bedrooms of the upper floor vacant. One day, one of the women went to fetch some clothing from the upper floor and discovered that the door to the stairwell was bolted from the inside.

Puzzled, she thought to herself, "Who could have bolted the door? Everyone is downstairs."

Finding a crack in the wall boards she peeked inside and saw a man sitting on the bed. She assumed he was a thief and promptly called for the rest of the family to come.

The man, however, said in a loud voice, "I am moving in to live on this floor and my family will soon be here to join me. I will borrow your beds and tables but the rest of your possessions will be returned immediately."

He thereupon threw various boxes and miscellaneous items out the window onto the ground below.

Not long after, the family heard a crowd of people milling about. They peeked through the wall boards and saw that the room was filled with people young and old. This crowd soon began clanking bowls and singing, "My lord, my kind host, you have guests who have come from afar but you have not provided even one glass of wine to welcome us."

In trepidation the family quickly prepared four tables with flagons of wine out in the courtyard, and all four tables were magically whisked upstairs. After the guests had feasted, they threw all the unwanted cutlery and china out the window. For a while after this there was no more obnoxious behavior.

All the same, this wealthy family decided it best to hire a Daoist priest to perform an exorcism. But in the midst of their discussions, the people upstairs began to sing, "Daoist dogs, Daoist dogs! Which of them would dare to deal with us?"

The next day a Daoist priest did come, but just as he was placing his exorcism paraphernalia on the altar, he appeared to be hit by something. He rushed out terrified and unsteady on his feet, his idols and instruments flying out behind him.

After this event there was no peace from the top floor, day or night, so eventually the owners went to Jiangxi to seek the assistance of the Daoist high priest, Zhang, who ordered one of his followers, a Daoist cleric, to perform the exorcism.

On hearing this news, the demons on the upper floor recommenced their singing: "High Priest, High Priest, your magic won't work on us. Daoist cleric, Daoist cleric, it's a waste of time for you to come."

Not long after this the cleric arrived, but suddenly, as if someone had grabbed him by the head, he was tossed to the ground, leaving his face bloodied and his clothes torn.

The cleric said with considerable shame, "These demons have tremendous power. We will succeed in expurgating them only if we obtain the assistance of the Reverend Xie."

The Reverend Xie resided in a temple in Chang'an County and was promptly invited to perform the exorcism. He erected an altar and began his task. This time the demons had not recommenced their singing and so the wealthy family were hopeful of success. Suddenly a streak of red light appeared in the sky and with it an old white-haired man.

This mysterious visitor went into the stairwell and called, "No need to be scared of this Daoist Xie. I can conquer his magic."

Xie sat at the front of the hall and began chanting his incantations, then threw a bowl onto the floor, where it ran along at a great speed. Several times it spun around the hall and then made as if to go up the stairs, but each time it failed. After a while the sound of bronze bells came from the upper floor, and with this the bowl immediately fell to the ground. No matter what he tried, Xie wasn't able to get it spinning again.

Startled, he said, "I've exhausted my powers. I can't exorcise these specters."

He thereupon picked up his bowl and left. From the upper floor came the sounds of great rejoicing and after this victory the specters' mischief reached unprecedented heights.

And so it continued for half a year, until one midwinter night there was a huge snowstorm. A dozen or so hunters came to the house requesting shelter and received the hesitant reply that although rooms were available, the house was plagued by demons.

One of the hunters replied, "I'll bet they're fox fairies. You know, hunting foxes is our speciality. Provide enough alcohol for us all to get drunk and we will repay you by driving those foxes out."

So the family supplied them with food and drink and the house remained brightly lit all night while the hunters reveled to their hearts' content. When they were all thoroughly drunk, they loaded their rifles with gunpowder and fired into the air. Smoke and dust billowed and a huge commotion ensued that lasted through the night. The family was extremely anxious lest this cause the demons to heighten their mischief making, but instead everything was quiet and peaceful by the next morning.

Several days passed and still not a sound was heard from the upper floor. The family decided to venture upstairs to investigate. They found the floor scattered with fur and all the windows flung wide open. The demons had gone.

張天師符

*The Daoist Cleric Zhang*

# *The Goats Who Fulfilled Their Fate*

In 1720, during the reign of the Kangxi emperor, the governor of Shandong, Li Shude, celebrated his birthday with an enormous party. He was showered with gifts of wine and goats by his subordinates, and the drinking, feasting, and entertainment continued unabated for several nights. Many guests didn't bother to sleep at all during this time.

One of them, a Mr. Zhang from the Bureau of Punishments, had had a little too much to drink and decided to retire to his quarters. As he entered his bedroom he heard from behind his bed curtain the groaning and whispering of a couple having sex. He assumed one of the other guests had availed himself of his bed to have some fun with a houseboy.

Zhang gave a shout and lifted the bed curtain only to find, making love on his bed just like a human couple, two of the white goats that had been presented to the governor as birthday gifts. When they saw Zhang, they jumped up in fright and trotted quickly away.

Zhang thought this hilarious and decided to tell his friends what he had just witnessed.

But before he could do so he collapsed senseless to the floor, began slapping himself about the face, and shouted abusively, "You old fool! You really are despicable! Mr. Xie and I are fated to be together through life and death.

"We were separated for four hundred and seventy years until we finally managed to get together today. Do you realize how difficult it was to arrange this meeting? Your interruption frightened us out of our wits, and what's more you've well and truly wrecked our betrothal plans. I'll have you know this is an unforgivable sin!"

Having finished this diatribe, Zhang recommenced slapping himself about the face.

The governor was quickly informed of this strange occurrence. He marched directly to the scene and said, "My dear Mistress Xie, why are you putting on such a performance? It's my birthday and I was planning on releasing all you animals to accumulate some virtue with the gods, so there really is no need for all this fuss. There are several hundred goats here, but I am sure that when I release you all into the wilderness, you'll each be able to find a suitable partner. I feel certain you'll be able to fulfill your destiny. Are you happy now?"

When the governor had finished speaking, Zhang said in a rather more compliant tone, "Thank you, my lord!" Zhang's body then jerked sharply and he was returned to his normal state.

It was Mr. Liang Yaofeng who told me of this incident.

# *Capturing a Ghost*

A certain Wang Qiming, formally of the riverside town of Wuyuan, decided to relocate his household farther up the river to an officer's lodge. This lodge had previously been the home of Qiming's clansman, a licensed scholar by the name of Wang Po.

One night in April 1774 Wang woke from a long and drawn-out nightmare to find a ghost pressing up against his bed curtains. This ghost was so huge that its head brushed the ceiling. But Wang was a brave and daring fellow, and he sprang up and launched a fierce attack on the ghost.

The terrified creature hastened to the door, but in its panic it crashed into the wall instead. Wang instantly seized the ghost round the waist and pinned it against the wall.

Instantly, an icy wind gusted up, extinguishing the bedside candles. When Wang turned back to look at the captured ghost its face had disappeared. Wang's hands were chilled to the bone, but he kept them clutched tightly around the ghost's trunklike midriff. He tried to call out to alert the household to his predicament but found himself paralyzed by the ghostly chill and unable to utter a sound.

Eventually Wang mustered all his strength and managed to scream for help. By the time his kinsfolk arrived the ghost had shrunk to the size of a newborn baby. A candle was brought over, and to everyone's surprise, clutched in Wang's hands was nothing more than a bundle of silk wadding.

At that instant the house was showered with broken bricks thrown from outside the bedroom window. Wang's kinsfolk were terrified at this display of ghostly wrath and begged Wang to release his grip on the wad of silk.

Wang laughed in reply. "Ghosts run around scaring people, but they're all bluff and bluster. What can they actually *do* to us? If I release this ghost, then I'd be rewarding the mischievous bullying of its friends. It's better to kill this ghost as a warning to all the others that we'll not suffer this type of intimidation."

Grasping the ghost's remains in his left hand, he took up a torch in his right and set about incinerating the wad of silk. It crackled and sparked in the heat and soon there spurted from the leaping flames fresh, scarlet blood. The stench of the fumes from this ghostly funeral pyre was almost unbearable.

At daybreak Wang's terrified neighbors crowded into the room to see the remains for themselves. The rising stench that assailed their nostrils was still so strong that they all hurried to cover their noses. Stinking, greasy blood the consistency of plaster lay an inch thick on the ground.

Nobody ever found out exactly what type of ghost it was that Wang had killed, and Wang Fengting, a local historian, simply recorded this event as "Capturing a Ghost."

# *Mr. Xu*

One of the wealthiest families in Susong County was that of Shi Zanchen. Moreover, Shi had several brothers and each of them was wealthy in his own right.

Susong County had a custom whereby wealthy households, like the Shi family, would set up a meal each day in their outer halls for whoever wished to come and partake. The name granted this custom was simply "the sitting-and-eating banquet."

One day a person by the name of Xu came to eat. He was slightly built and wore a scanty beard. While eating, he pointed at the green hill beyond the gate and said, "Has anyone seen a hill jump before?"

The unanimous reply was, "Never!"

Xu then pointed at the hill three times and the hill did indeed jump three times. His audience was greatly surprised, but even more mystified at Mr. Xu's powers. He was thereafter respectfully called Venerable Master.

One day, Master Xu said to Shi, "Although your family is already very wealthy, I can increase your wealth tenfold by smelting gold from silver with Daoist magic."

The Shi brothers were rather suspicious of his claim but decided they had little to lose, and so they had a furnace built and each contributed several thousand taels of silver hoping to have it transformed into gold. The wife of the second brother was a very sneaky woman and, unknown to the Venerable Master, mixed some copper among the silver. When the fire had burned down to ash, a huge bolt of lightning hit the house with a tremendous crack, smashing several roof tiles.

The Venerable Master cursed. "Somebody must have sneaked fake silver into the furnace. This deception has made the gods extremely angry."

After some discussion the Shis uncovered the wife's trick and their respect for Master Xu's magical powers increased enormously.

Another time the Venerable Master threw a copper basin into midair and shouted, "Come hither, coins!" A coin promptly dropped into the basin. He continued his shouting and soon the air was filled with the noise of coins of all shapes and sizes hitting the basin.

The Venerable Master then said, "If we go deep into the hills, far from human habitation, we will be able to make a huge basin and become tremendously rich. Why don't you come with me to Mount Lu, over in Jiangxi Province?"

The Shi brothers were ecstatic. Pooling their finances, they followed the Venerable Master forth.

Halfway there, the Venerable Master went ashore. That night he led several dozen bandits wielding great torches and clubs to rob the brothers of their silver.

He said to the brothers, "Don't be frightened. Although I am the leader of this gang, I do have a conscience. You have treated me well, so if you hand over your silver without a fuss, I'll let you all return home unharmed."

So the Shi brothers gave him everything they had and shamefacedly returned home.

Ten years later, a messenger from the Anqing police headquarters arrived with a summons for Shi Zanchen. "We have imprisoned a great robber by the name of Xu and he has requested to see you before he is executed."

Shi had no choice but to go. Upon his arrival he found that it was indeed Master Xu.

The Venerable Master said, "I have a request to ask of you, Zanchen. My time is drawing to a close, but I have no regrets about dying, and considering the length of our friendship, I want you to be responsible for burying my body."

He took four gold bracelets from his wrist and passed them to Shi on the understanding that these would cover any funeral expenses. Then he said, "My execution is set for the afternoon of July the first. You may come and bid me farewell then."

At the appointed execution time Shi went to the central market square in Anqing, where he saw the Venerable Master with his hands tied behind his back awaiting decapitation. Suddenly, a small child dropped from Shi's crotch and said in the voice of the Venerable Master, "Watch me being killed! Watch me being killed!"

In that instant, Xu's head fell to the ground and the child disappeared as suddenly and as mysteriously as it had appeared.

The executioner at the time was Zu Tinggui, a Manchu of the blue banner.

# *The Hairy People of Qin*

In Yunyang's Fang County, on the border between the provinces of Hunan and Guangdong, there is a mountain of enormous magnitude called House Peak. Its name is derived from the roomlike caves that flank its four sides. Its height and isolation make it treacherous to venture near.

Living in this mountain are a people whose bodies are covered with hair and who measure over ten feet. Every so often they venture from the mountain to steal the nearby villagers' livestock for food. If anyone dared to try to prevent this theft, the hairy people would retaliate while retreating with the animals they had snatched. Firearms provided no protection since the lead shot would simply bounce off the hairy people and fall to the ground, leaving them completely unharmed. Traditional wisdom maintains there is only one way of preventing their rampages, and that is to clap your hands and shout, "Build a great wall! Build a great wall!" On hearing this, the hairy people run away in terror.

A lifelong friend of mine by the name of Zhang Qun held an official post in this region and his experience confirms the efficacy of this tactic.

The locals explained the phenomenon thus: "In the Qin dynasty during the building of the Great Wall, some of the villagers avoided conscription by hiding in the mountains. After many years they evolved into these strange hairy creatures. We noticed that whenever they came into contact with other people, they would ask whether the Great Wall was completed, thereby exposing their weak point and enabling us to frighten them away."

One can appreciate how fierce the emperor of Qin must have been if after several thousand years these people still lived in terror of Qin laws.

# *The Human Ape*

In Keerke, Xinjiang, there lived a type of animal that looked very similar to an ape but was in fact no ape at all. The Chinese living in the region called these creatures "human apes" and the locals named them *geli.* The human apes would often poke their heads into people's tents begging for food and drink, or sometimes even asking for small household items like knives or tobacco. The usual response was to shout loudly at these creatures, sending them scampering away.

A general stationed in the region managed to domesticate one of these human apes and eventually trained it to perform simple household chores, like fetching water and grinding flour. Indeed, this creature served the general well for just on a year. The time came, however, for the general to complete his tour of duty in Xinjiang and return to China. On the day of the general's departure, the human ape stood in front of his master's horse weeping copiously. Then, as the party moved off, the creature followed along behind for over ten miles, quite clearly miserable at the idea of being parted from the general.

The general eventually turned to the creature and said, "You can't come back to China with me, just as I can't live here forever in your country. You must stop following me now!" The human ape gave out a pitiful howl, and although he dutifully ceased his pursuit, his eyes never left the general until his mounted figure had faded into the distance.

# *The Human Prawn*

At the beginning of the current dynasty there lived an old man who wanted to make the ultimate sacrifice—taking his own life—to display his unbounded loyalty to the previous Ming dynasty. He was, however, too scared to commit suicide. He didn't fancy the idea of using a knife, nor did he care for the idea of hanging himself. Incineration was similarly unappealing.

Eventually, he struck upon the notion of emulating a certain Minister Xinling, who had apparently committed suicide by indulging in an excess of wine and women. Thus resolved, our Ming loyalist brought in several concubines and mistresses and thereafter indulged himself in unlimited lascivious pursuits.

This went on for years, yet still he showed no signs of dying from his excesses. The only effects on his body were that his nerves were shot, his head protruded at an unusual angle, and his back developed a hump. Indeed, he was so badly hunched over that he looked for all the world like a giant cooked prawn.

His crooked gait was almost a crawl on all fours, so people in the region called him the Human Prawn. He stayed in this prawnlike state for over twenty years and died at the ripe old age of eighty-four. My friend Wang Zijian told me that he had seen this old man with his very own eyes when he was just a young boy.

## *The Duck's Lover*

In Jiangxi's Gaoan County there was a young man by the name of Yang Gui. Now Yang Gui was a slim and extremely attractive nineteen-year-old. He was mild in manner, compliant by nature, and never known to refuse sexual advances of any sort.

One summer's day he was bathing in the village pond when a drake flew up at him from the water and bit him on the buttocks. The drake then whacked Yang with his tail and made humping movements over Yang's buttocks. Yang tried to fend off the duck, beating it repeatedly, but the duck persisted. It wasn't long before Yang had beaten it to death. When he examined the limp body floating in the water, he saw protruding from among the tail feathers a fleshy stalk. Around the stalk the water was murky with some sort of emission.

The locals thought this episode absolutely hilarious, and from then on Yang Gui became known as the Duck's Lover.

# *The Spirit of the Turtle Stone*

In Wuxi there lived a very handsome, refined young scholar by the name of Hua. He and his family lived along the banks of a river, near a Confucian temple. Directly in front of this temple was a grand bridge that had become a favorite resting place for travelers. One summer day, Hua also sought respite from the heat in the cool of the bridge.

Later in the afternoon as he strolled towards his college he noticed a young woman leaning against the side gate of a nearby lane. His interest was aroused and he wandered over to chat. The woman smiled as he drew near and they eyed each other appreciatively. Hua was just about to engage her in conversation when she suddenly went inside and closed the gate. Before going on his way, Hua made a mental note of the location of her lane.

The next day he returned to the lane and found the woman waiting. Upon inquiry, Hua found she was the daughter of a college caretaker. She then added, "My lodgings are too cramped for a private tryst, but your house is close by. So if you can arrange a secluded room, I will come and spend the nights with you. Wait for me tomorrow evening at your gate."

Our young man gleefully returned home and instructed the housekeepers to prepare the outer room, telling his wife that he would prefer to sleep outside to avoid the heat. That night, in great stealth, he waited by the gate and surely enough the young woman appeared. They walked hand in hand into the outer room and spent a night together that exceeded Hua's wildest expectations. From hereon in she paid him a visit every night.

After several months of this nightly activity Hua grew pale and thin. His parents suspected that something was amiss and they decided one night to stay up and check on him. When they discovered him making merry in the company of a young woman they pushed open the door and rushed in, but in a flash the woman had gone. They interrogated their son, whereupon he confessed to his liaison and narrated the entire sequence of events that had led to his current state of ill health.

His parents were horrified. The next day they accompanied Hua to his college to look for the woman. But the gate he had described was nowhere to be found and none of the college caretakers was known to have a daughter fitting the woman's description. It became apparent the woman they were dealing with was some sort of spirit, so they immediately sought the advice of monks and priests.

The spirit-repelling charms and talismans that they received proved useless, however. Finally Hua's parents gave him some cinnabar and told him, "When she returns tonight, rub some of this onto her. That way we will be able to trace her movements tomorrow." That night, while the couple lay together, Hua secretly rubbed the cinnabar into her hair.

The next day, the young man and his parents went to the Confucian temple to search for traces of red dust, but not a spot could be found. Suddenly they heard a woman scolding her young boy, "I just put a clean pair of pants on you and now you've got them covered in red dirt! Where on earth have you been playing?"

Hua's father's suspicions were immediately aroused and he went to have a look at the child's trousers. They were indeed covered in cinnabar. He asked where the boy had been playing and the child pointed toward the turtle statue under the college stele. "I was just riding on the turtle's head. I didn't mean to get dirty."

On examining the turtle statue they discovered that it was covered in cinnabar, so they immediately notified the college authorities and the turtle was duly destroyed. Among the splinters of rock from the smashed statue were traces of blood, and in the rubble lay a gleaming, egg-shaped pebble. It was so dense that no one was able to smash it, so they simply threw it into Lake Tai. For a while after this the woman did not return.

Half a month later, however, she reappeared in the young man's bedroom, complaining loudly about the injustice she had suffered. "What crime have I committed to deserve the destruction of my old form? All the same I'm not angry—your parents were only acting out of concern for your health. Look, I have begged some herbs from an immortal that are certain to cure you." She produced several grassy leaves and forced Hua to take them. They were sweet and fragrant.

Then she said, "Before, when I lived nearby, it was very easy to make my nightly visits. But my new form is much farther away and it will be impossible for me to travel to and fro, so I will have to reside here with you." And so she joined the household, although she never partook of food or drink.

Everyone in the family could see her, and Hua's wife openly abused her. But on such occasions the woman would just smile silently. Each evening, Hua's wife would sit on the bed with her arms protectively around her husband, intending to prevent the woman from sharing their bed. The woman, for her part, did not force the issue. Instead she would wait until the wife was sound asleep and oblivious to the world before joining Hua in bed. She could thus enjoy him all for herself. After Hua had taken the herbs, not only did his former good health return but he was also protected from the wasting sickness that had plagued him during his earlier sexual encounters with the woman. His parents could do nothing but let the woman have her way, and so it continued for over a year.

One day Hua chanced upon a scabby Daoist monk. After scrutinizing Hua the monk announced, "I can see that you are possessed. You had better tell me the truth or your end will be nigh!" The young man told him the whole story and the scabby monk then invited him to a teahouse, where he promptly swung a gourd over his shoulder and took a swig of wine. He then gave the young scholar two yellow paper charms. "Take these home and paste one onto the door of your bedroom and the other onto your bed. Don't tell the woman of this. Your fate is not yet sealed. On the fifteenth day of the eighth month I will pay you a visit." It was then the middle of the sixth month.

On returning home, he pasted the charms in the designated places. When the woman returned she was shocked and cursed him. "Why have you become so coldhearted again? You can't frighten me with these!" Although her tone was harsh and defiant, she dared not enter the room.

After a long while she laughed loudly. "I have a choice of the utmost gravity for you to make. If you are interested in hearing it you must first rid the bedroom of these charms." He did as requested and she entered the room. "You are an attractive man. I love you and want you to be my husband. The Daoist monk also loves you but he wants you to be his acolyte and lover. Which one of us will you choose?" Hua was horrified to think that the monk had such an ulterior motive. Thus persuaded, he and the woman resumed their romance.

One midautumn evening Hua and the young woman were gazing at the full moon when they were interrupted by someone calling Hua's name. In the darkness Hua could see that the voice belonged to someone standing just beyond the wall. He hurried over and recognized the man to be the scabby monk. The monk took him by the arm and said, "The ghost's life is drawing to a close. I have come here especially to exorcise her from your household." It became apparent from the young man's expression that he was not very pleased with this news and so the monk continued. "I know that the ghost has slandered me. For this I am even less inclined to forgive her." He wrote out another two charms for Hua and said, "Quick! Go and capture her!"

The young man turned to go, but then hesitated and finally stopped. So his parents, who had come out to see what was happening, carried the charms to his wife's residence instead. Hua's wife was ecstatic. Holding the charms, she walked towards the woman, who shook and shivered in fright. They then bound the woman's hands and carried her outside.

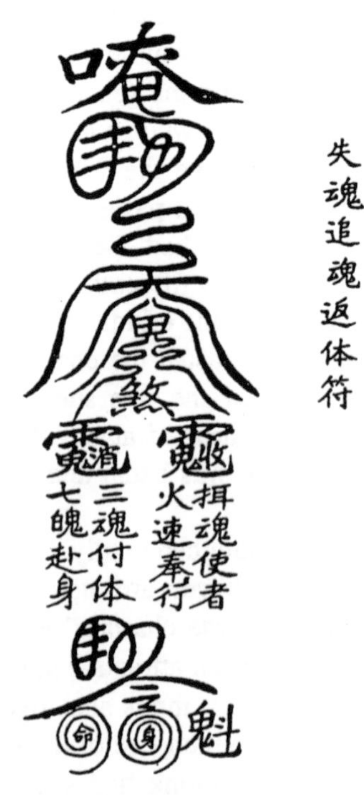


*Magical Charm*

The woman wept and pleaded with Hua. "I knew that my life was nearly over and I know that I should have left before, but I was so deeply in love with you that I kept delaying my departure. Now this calamity has befallen me. I have loved you dearly all these years and soon we will be parted forever. I beg you to put me in the shade of the wall, away from the moonlight, so that I might be reprieved of my death sentence. Have pity on me, will you?"

The young man did not have the heart to see her die in such misery, so he carried her to the shaded side of the wall and untied her hands. The woman promptly leaped into the air and was transformed into a streak of black smoke that sped through the sky. The Daoist monk immediately let out a shrill cry and gave chase through the air to the southeast.

Nobody knows what became of them.

# *Ghosts Who Play with Firecrackers May Burn Themselves*

In Shaoxing there was a mansion that remained, on its owner's instructions, locked fast. It happened one day that a traveler came by seeking lodgings for the night.

The owner of the mansion informed him, "You are quite welcome to rent the eastern mansion, but you do so at your own peril."

Our traveler inquired as to the meaning of this cryptic welcome and was told, "The building was previously used for storage, and my two servants were quartered there. Late one evening we were disturbed in our nighttime preparations by a frightful howling from the mansion. We rushed over and found the servants pale and shaking, speechless with fear. It was quite some time before they regained their composure.

"They later told me, 'Just before we had blown the candle out in preparation for sleep, a creature in the form of a huge stone monument came to our bedside, opened the bed curtain, and made as if to join us. Frightened beyond belief, we ran from the building screaming. This is the truth for we saw this creature with our own eyes.' Naturally, after this strange event no one has dared live in that building."

After hearing the owner reach the end of his tale our traveler simply laughed and said, "I'll give it a try."

His host tried in vain to dissuade him from such a reckless course, but in the end he was compelled to sweep out the dust, put down some mats, and prepare the building for residence.

On entering his temporary home the traveler, armed with his sword, went directly to the top floor. There he lit a candle and waited.

Finally, in the deep of the night, his patience was rewarded by a rustling sound emanating from the northern end of the room. He gazed in that direction and in the gloom made out the form of the ghost. It looked just as the landlord had described.

The ghost jumped onto a chair and began examining some books that had been left on the table. Soon wearying of this pastime, the ghost proceeded to empty the contents of our traveler's luggage onto the table and inspect them one by one.

Among the various items of personal use were several batches of Huizhou firecrackers. These the demon scrutinized attentively in the light of a lamp, which by curious coincidence happened to spit a spark onto the wick of the firecrackers.

This, of course, caused a thunderous explosion, which left the ghost momentarily rolling around the floor blubbering before taking its chance to disappear.

Our traveler was greatly puzzled by these antics. Suspecting that the demon would return, he maintained his vigil until dawn. There were no more visitations, however; not a trace of the demon was seen.

In amazement the traveler narrated the night's events to his landlord, who was equally perplexed. The following night our traveler returned to the upper floor of the mansion and passed the night without incident or evidence of supernatural presence.

From that day on, the building was free from strange events and accompanying ghosts.

# *Kaxiong*

Yang Kaxiong was orphaned at an early age when his father died unexpectedly during garrison duty. The boy's distant uncle, a Mr. Zhou, was a vice-commander of the military stationed in Hezhou. Taking pity on the orphan, Zhou decided to raise Kaxiong as his own child.

Zhou had a daughter who was approximately the same age as Kaxiong, and seeing that Kaxiong was young, intelligent, and handsome, she took a liking to him.

The Zhou family were very strict on matters of social decorum and consequently the young couple's contact was limited to formal family dining.

Another relative, a young man by the name of Wu, was also supported by the Zhous, and he slept outside in the study.

One autumn night when Kaxiong felt insufferably hot he took a stroll under the moonlight to enjoy the cool night air. In the distance he saw the young Miss Zhou strolling towards him. By the end of the night the couple had become extremely intimate.

The next day he chanced upon her in the midst of her morning toilet but they simply exchanged smiles. From hereon in she visited him every night.

On one of these occasions Wu was disturbed by the sound of laughter coming from Kaxiong's quarters and he grew suspicious. Peeking inside, he saw Miss Zhou and Kaxiong engaged in sexual intercourse and this made him extremely jealous.

He resolved to pass this information on to Mr. Zhou. On hearing about his daughter's conduct, Mr. Zhou immediately went to the inner quarters and scolded his wife for her laxity.

In her defense Mrs. Zhou said, "How could this be? Our daughter shares my bed every night."

Zhou was still unconvinced so he found an excuse to cane Kaxiong and drove him out of the house.

Having nobody else but the Zhous to rely on, Kaxiong took refuge in an ancient temple in Lanzhou. It wasn't long before Miss Zhou appeared at the temple carrying her luxurious luggage.

Kaxiong was overjoyed and asked how she had managed to find him.

"I came with my uncle Wu." Then she explained to Kaxiong that Mr. Zhou's younger brother, Wu, had just been promoted to the post of military commander in Lanzhou.

Kaxiong had no reason to doubt her words and proceeded to set up house with her for a few weeks. They lived in grand style and were blissfully happy.

One day not long after this Miss Zhou's uncle bumped into Kaxiong on the street and greeted him cheerfully. "So you're here as well, nephew!" Kaxiong amiably replied in the affirmative. The two men rode back to Kaxiong's residence, where they were greeted by Zhou's daughter.

The uncle was puzzled by her presence, so Kaxiong explained what had happened. The uncle thought to himself, "My brother made no mention of his daughter's absence to me. Perhaps he was too ashamed to mention it?"

He stayed with the young couple for several days and then, using the opportunity provided by military business, paid a visit to his brother in Hezhou.

Zhou, informed about his brother's encounter with his daughter, was incredulous. "This is impossible! My daughter is this very moment in her chamber quite safe and sound. In fact she'll be joining us for dinner in a short while. Perhaps your Miss Zhou is a fox fairy who is impersonating my daughter."

Zhou's wife said, "This fox fairy will blacken the family name by pretending to be our daughter and carrying on in this way. Why don't we present our real daughter to Kaxiong for marriage and see what happens then?"

The two brothers thought this a superb idea and immediately began the betrothal arrangements.

On the eve of the wedding Kaxiong returned to his room and was stunned to see his bride-to-be already there.

The woman smiled and said, "Why are you so flustered?" She then related the following story.

"I am a fox and I have come to repay a debt of gratitude for a kindness your father once bestowed upon me.

"When your father the general was alive he often went hunting and one day I was shot by his arrow. Instead of killing me he pulled the arrow out and set me free. Since that day I have been seeking a way to repay his kindness and today I have succeeded.

"When I discovered that you were having difficulty realizing your love for Miss Zhou, I decided to become your matchmaker and help you achieve your desire. Of course, if you and Miss Zhou had not already been destined for each other, I would have been unable to help.

"Now that my matchmaking is done, I will leave."

And with this she disappeared.

## *Freak Wind*

The Dajing military camp was based in Liangzhou at Mount Song, in the middle of a gravelly desert. The site was that of an old battlefield, and one day General Ta Siha led his troops farther into the desert on routine surveillance.

As far as his eyes could see the landscape was barren, spotted here and there with low scrub and disturbed only by wisps of yellow dust.

Suddenly a huge mountain reared up from the ground, eventually blocking out the sun. As it rose before them, the terrified soldiers and their startled horses could hear a tremendous crackling and thunderous roars.

General Ta was just as frightened as his men, particularly when he noticed that the mountain was advancing towards them.

It approached so quickly that there was no hope of escape. So the men leaped off their horses, formed a tight circle, closed their eyes, and waited for the worst.

Seconds later they were enveloped in pitch darkness. The men and their horses were knocked to the ground and tossed around mercilessly by this dark force for quite some time. But eventually all was calm once again.

The entire troop of thirty-six men emerged covered in blood with little pebbles embedded in their skin, some half an inch deep. When they turned to look at the departing mountain, it was already dozens of miles in the distance.

That evening they returned to the Dajing base camp and reported this phenomenon to the chief of staff, Ma Chenghu.

Ma laughed at General Ta, saying, "That wasn't a mountain! It was just a freak windstorm. You'd all be dead now if it had really been a mountain.

"This sort of windstorm occurs quite regularly out there during the winter months. You've all survived the storm, but it's obvious your faces are badly pockmarked by the flying stones.

"The scars will probably be permanent, so I suggest you make sure the troop's personnel records are updated to incorporate these changes to your men's appearances."

# *The Old Woman Who Was Transformed into a Wolf*

In Aizhou County, Guangdong Province, there was a peasant by the name of Sun, whose mother had lived well into her seventies. One day, completely out of the blue, she started to grow hair on her arms. The hair spread to her back and then to her stomach and hands. Eventually she was entirely covered with inch-long hair. It was then that her body began to shrivel and a tail began to grow from her buttocks. Soon after the tail had formed she collapsed to the ground and before everyone's eyes was transformed into a white-haired wolf.

The wolf dashed out of the house and was gone. There was nothing the startled Sun family could do but wait to see if she would return. As it turned out, the wolf returned regularly, once every three or four weeks. She would check on her sons and grandchildren and would usually have a meal and a drink before leaving again.

The neighbors were disgusted by this unnatural creature and threatened to kill her, or at least drive her away from the village. Her son and his wife were terrified that something would indeed befall their mother if she continued to visit, so they resolved to warn her against returning. They prepared a banquet with delicacies such as pig trotters, and when the wolf next returned, her son explained that the feast was in her honor.

"Mother, after this feast is over you must never come home again. We know that you think of us while you're out in the woods, and we know that you would never do anyone any harm, but the neighbors are fearful. They are planning to kill you and have their weapons ready at this very moment. We would never be able to live with ourselves if you were killed paying us a visit. So please, stay away and keep yourself safe."

On hearing their advice the wolf howled mournfully, but then, after one last look at her loved ones, she ran off into the forest and was never seen again.

# *A Loyal Dog Makes Use of Another Dog's Body*

An exceptionally handsome young Peking man named Chang had a dog by the name of Flower on whom he doted. Chang and Flower were inseparable—wherever Chang went, Flower could be seen scampering along behind.

One fine spring day they went to Fengtai to view the park's famous blossoms. By the time they began their homeward journey it was late and there were very few people around.

Unfortunately, as Chang and Flower made their way through the empty grounds they happened to pass three noisy young hooligans stretched out on the grass drinking.

Now these three young drunks decided to have some fun with the handsome young man, and they began yelling all sorts of obscene propositions.

When the drunks received no response they switched to more direct tactics. They jumped at Chang and started kissing him and pulling his clothes off. Young Chang was absolutely mortified, both embarrassed and terrified at this assault. He tried to struggle free, but he wasn't very strong and was clearly outnumbered.

Seeing her master in strife, Flower growled and rushed in to bite the attackers. One of the young hooligans turned his attention to Flower, stoning the dog and eventually smashing her skull.

Flower sank to the ground beneath a nearby tree, dead.

Having rid themselves of this nuisance, the three hooligans set upon Chang with greater seriousness of purpose. They bound his arms and legs with his belt, pulled his trousers down to his knees and then pushed him face down to the ground. Two of the youths held Chang down while the other ripped his own trousers off and thrust himself down onto Chang's buttocks, intending to sodomize the helpless young man.

Suddenly, out of the bushes rushed a mangy dog. He bit the rapist right on the testicles and with a quick twist of his neck ripped them off. Then, dropping the bleeding sacs to the ground, the dog escaped back into the bushes. Blood gushed from the wounded man's groin, and his friends, in terror lest the dog return, carried him home.

Eventually passersby saw Chang tied up on the ground. They undid the belt, helped him dress himself, and saw him on his way home.

In the quiet of his own residence, Chang felt the loss of his loyal dog more keenly than before. He vowed to return the next day to retrieve Flower's body so as to give her a proper burial.

That night he dreamed that Flower spoke to him: "You have always been so kind to me. I was robbed of my chance to repay this kindness when that villain killed me. But even though I was physically dead, my soul was very much alive.

"I attached myself to the body of the mangy dog that lives at the bean curd store, and was able to kill that rapist all the same. Now, even though I am dead, I can rest in peace knowing I have served you well." Flower then whimpered pitifully before disappearing.

The next day Chang went to the bean curd store to see if there really were such a mangy dog. The dog did indeed exist, and when Chang asked the owner about it he was told, "This dog is really sick, old, and quite incapable of biting anyone. But you know, last night he came home with his mouth dripping with blood. I'm still not sure what happened."

Chang then sent some friends to ask about recent deaths in the locality, and sure enough the young hooligan had died of his wounds the previous night soon after returning home.

# *Leng Qiujiang*

In 1745 a Zhenjiang silk merchant by the name of Cheng was returning home one night through the foothills of Elephant Mountain. At one particularly isolated place along the road, a small child ran out from the bushes and graves scattered around and tugged at his clothes.

Cheng knew it was a ghost and shouted at it, but it refused to leave. Not long afterwards, another small child ran up and clutched Cheng's hand.

The first child then tried to pull Cheng westward towards a wall crowded with shadows. Suddenly he found himself pelted with mud.

Then the second child pulled him eastward towards another wall from which came some ghostly sounds. This time Cheng was pelted with gravel.

Cheng was powerless and had to submit to the pushing and pulling of the children. From both sides the ghosts began to jeer at him, and then they appeared to fight over him among themselves. Cheng was terrified and finally collapsed in a heap in the mud, prepared for the worst.

Suddenly a ghost cried out, "Master Leng is coming. We must get out of his way! He may be learned, but he's thoroughly detestable and awfully obstinate nonetheless!"

Surely enough, striding jauntily along the track with his shoulders pushed back, came a large man. He was beating a large fan against the palm of his hand to keep time as he sang, "The river flows eastward." He lumbered towards Cheng, showing not the least bit of fear, and the ghosts instantly scattered.

This man looked down at Cheng and smiled. "Are those vile ghosts harassing you? Worry no longer. I'm here to save you, so just walk along with me now."

Cheng duly rose and followed him.

All the while the man kept up his singing and after they had walked several miles the sky began to lighten. He turned to Cheng and said, "We are close to your home now, so I'll be off."

Cheng bowed, thanked him, and asked his name, to which he received the reply "I am Leng Qiujiang, and I live at the crossroads of the east gate."

On arriving back home, Cheng discovered that his nostrils, mouth, ears, indeed every possible orifice, had been filled with dark mud. His startled family hastily washed him down with herbal water. Once more in a presentable state he decided to go over to the east gate to express his gratitude to his rescuer.

At the crossroads he discovered that there was no one by the name of Leng Qiujiang to be found.

After extensive inquiries he was told, "There is an ancestral temple here for the Leng family and inside you'll find that there's a tablet for someone by the name of Mei. This fellow was a scholar in the early Shunzhi era and he had the literary title Qiujiang."

# *The Nailed-up Specter Makes Good Her Escape*

In Jurong County there was a bounty hunter by the name of Yin Qian who was famous for his success in apprehending thieves. His technique involved lurking in the dark recesses of the village while waiting for his prey to pass. Then, when the thief least expected it, Yin Qian would leap out and make his arrest.

One day as he was walking towards the village, a person carrying a length of rope brushed past him in a hurry. Yin suspected criminal intent so he followed the figure to the outside of a house. His quarry then jumped a short wall and entered the courtyard.

Yin thought to himself, "I probably won't get any bounty payment if I hand this fellow over to the authorities, but if I wait a while I may be able get my reward by relieving him of his loot."

A short while later Yin's suspicions were aroused when he detected the muffled sounds of a woman crying. He promptly jumped the wall and from his vantage point in the courtyard observed a seated woman staring at her likeness in a bedroom mirror.

Also visible to Yin was a woman with matted hair who was balancing on the roof beam directly above the seated lady, trying to catch her with a noosed rope.

Yin realized instantly that he had stumbled upon the ghost of a woman who had hanged herself, and that the ghost was trying to find a replacement soul. With a great shout he threw open the gates and burst into the house. All the various members of the household, and even some of the neighbors, came running to see the cause of the commotion and listened in surprise as Yin explained.

When they checked on the woman in question, they did indeed find her hanging by the neck from a rope attached to the roof beam. They quickly untied the rope and set about reviving her. To display the depth of their gratitude, the woman's father-in-law and aunts held a sumptuous banquet in Yin's honor.

When the feast had ended, Yin set off for home along the same road he had traveled earlier in the day. It was not yet light when he heard behind him a rustling sound. He turned and saw the very same ghost following him, still clutching her rope.

The ghost cursed him. "I was going to take that woman. It was none of your business! Why did you break my spell?" Using all her strength, she then tried to tie up Yin with her rope.

Yin was a courageous fellow and he tried to fight her off. Curiously, whenever his fist hit the ghost it was enveloped in an eerie chill that carried the sickly stench of blood.

As the sky lightened the ghost, still bearing her rope, began to tire. Yin, on the contrary, found his strength and courage increasing. Seizing this opportunity, he grabbed the ghost and tightened his grip.

An early-morning passerby was treated to the spectacle of Yin discharging an incessant barrage of abuse at a piece of rotten wood he was clutching to his chest. Drawing nearer, our curious passerby saw Yin shake himself, as if waking from slumber, and then drop the piece of wood to the ground.

Yin was incensed and explained that a ghost had lodged itself inside that particular piece of wood. He declared, "I won't let this block of wood get off so lightly."

On returning home he promptly nailed it to a post in his courtyard, and each night thereafter he would hear cries of pain and sounds of piteous weeping coming from the post.

Several days later, Yin's courtyard was filled by a group of people whose object was to persuade Yin to show clemency towards the ghost. From their childlike, screechy voices Yin concluded that these were fellow ghosts and promptly disregarded their pleas for mercy.

One of these ghosts shouted to the block of wood, "Lucky his lordship only nailed you up. If he'd tied you with rope you'd really be in pain."

At this, the other ghosts bristled and muttered, "Be quiet! Don't say things like that! What if Yin heard you?"

Later, Yin exchanged the nails for a rope. That night the courtyard was free of weeping and wailing.

When Yin examined the piece of wood the following day, it was clear the ghost had made good her escape.

# *The Messenger of Death Who Loved His Wine*

In Hangzhou there lived a man by the name of Yuan Guanlan, who remained unmarried well into his forties. His neighbor's daughter, however, took a liking to him despite his age. He thought she was an attractive girl, and soon their love grew.

When Guanlan mentioned the possibility of marriage to his beloved's father, however, it was opposed on the grounds that Guanlan was too poor to marry. The daughter pined for her lover and it wasn't long before she had died from misery.

Guanlan heard the news of his beloved's death and was stricken with grief. He wandered sadly out into the moonlit night and bought some wine to drown his sorrows.

He had been drinking for only a short time when he saw a dim figure leaning up against a wall. The person had disheveled hair and held a rope in its hand that was tied to something out of Guanlan's view.

The person smiled at him, and Guanlan, assuming the man to be a servant of one of his neighbors, waved and said, "Would you care to share my wine?"

The person nodded and a cup of wine was duly poured for him. The strange thing was, this man didn't drink in the normal fashion. Instead of drinking through his mouth, he sniffed the wine up his nose.

Guanlan worried that the wine might not be warm enough for his guest and so he asked, "Is this too cold for you?"

The man nodded, and Guanlan warmed a second cup for him. This time the cup was emptied with one snort of the mighty nostrils. Guanlan poured more wine.

The more wine the stranger sniffed up, the redder his face became, until eventually Guanlan's guest was incapable of holding his mouth closed. Guanlan then poured the wine straight down the gaping throat.

It wasn't long before he noticed that with each swig of wine the stranger's body grew smaller, until after a bottle he had shrunk to the size of a newborn baby and lay paralyzed on the ground.

Guanlan pulled at the rope the man had been holding. To his great surprise he discovered his neighbor's daughter, his dead lover, tied to the end. Guanlan was ecstatic and moved quickly to rid himself of the drunken messenger of death. He pushed the shrunken form into his wine jug, sealed the top, and trapped it by writing a hexagram on the lid. He untied his beloved and drew her into his bedroom, where they became husband and wife in all but name. From then on they lived a contented life, although not quite a regular one. During the night Guanlan's new wife had a visible form, but during the day she disappeared and could only be heard, not seen.

This situation continued for about a year, until one day she said gleefully to Guanlan, "I have been given permission to be reborn. Just wait, I'll become the most beautiful wife you have ever dreamed of.

"A young woman in the next village is going to die tomorrow, so I'll go over and borrow her body for my reincarnation. You must go to

*Messenger from the Underworld*

their house and claim to be able to revive their daughter in exchange for a reward. The cash will come in handy for our wedding expenses."

That very next day, Guanlan went to the village and located the bereaved family. The parents were sobbing with grief as they prepared for the funeral. Guanlan called to them, "I have some medicine that will bring her back to life. I'll give it to her if you let me take her as my wife when she recovers."

Naturally the family agreed, so Guanlan leaned over the corpse and whispered in its ear. This whispering went on for a little while and eventually the dead woman sat up large as life. The watching villagers were sure it was the work of a god, but a deal was a deal, so Guanlan and his reincarnated wife were married.

Strangely, for a year after her reincarnation Guanlan's wife remembered only the past of the daughter whose body she had borrowed. She regained the memories of her own family only gradually.

Best of all, the newly reincarnated wife was much better looking than the original wife!

# *A Fox Fairy Plays Guanyin for Three Years*

A scholar by the name of Zhou from Hangzhou was walking with the grand Daoist master Zhang one day. The two men stopped at an inn in Baoding, and there appeared a beautiful woman who knelt on the steps in front of the grand master. She looked as if she was praying.

The scholar then asked the grand master what had happened between them and the master replied, "That woman is a fox fairy. She was just asking me permission to use some incense from the human world, that's all."

The scholar asked in reply, "Did you grant her wish?"

Grand Master Zhang replied, "She has been cultivating her spirit for years and I can detect a distinct spiritual aura around her. I am rather concerned that if I give her some of the potent incense she requested, she'll have the magical power to turn herself into an object of worship."

Now Scholar Zhou rather fancied the looks of the young woman, so he persuaded Zhang to grant her permission to use the incense.

The grand master responded, "You have put me in a very awkward position, as I have no desire to deny your wishes. I'll give her permission to use this incense for three years, but she must receive no more after this period is over."

Having thus decided, Grand Master Zhang ordered one of his priests to put the agreement in writing on his yellow paper and pass it on to the young woman.

Three years later, just after Scholar Zhou had failed the imperial examinations, he made his way from the capital and passed through Suzhou. There he heard that on a nearby mountain, there was a temple to the goddess Guanyin where miraculous events were happening. In his despondent state he decided to make his way up to the temple to offer some prayers and leave a few offerings.

At the base of the mountain he made inquiries and was told by several fellow pilgrims, "This particular Guanyin achieves remarkable results, but you have to walk up, you can't go by sedan chair. Everyone who tries to go by sedan chair encounters problems and ends up walking."

This advice seemed too fanciful for our scholar to believe, so he set off in a sedan chair. But after a mere ten or so paces, the poles on the chair snapped and he tumbled to the ground. Fortunately he wasn't injured. Rather chastened, he continued on foot.

On reaching the temple, Zhou could see it was well patronized. Offerings and incense filled the altars. It appeared the so-called Guanyin was seated behind some silk drapes, which concealed her from view.

When Scholar Zhou asked the reason for this strange custom, an attendant monk replied, "Our Guanyin is so beautiful that we fear people will be driven to unholy thoughts and deeds if they look upon her form."

*Guanyin, Goddess of Mercy*

Scholar Zhou was not satisfied with this answer and insisted upon seeing the Guanyin without the curtains. The voluptuous vision he saw before him really was quite unlike any other Guanyin he had ever seen.

The longer he looked, the more familiar the face appeared. Finally it dawned on him that this was the same woman on whose behalf he had interceded three years previously at the inn.

Outraged, he pointed at the statue, saying, "Three years ago I spoke on your behalf in good faith. Now you have this bounty of offerings and incense and what do I receive in return? Not only did you not thank me, but today you broke my sedan chair. What sort of gratitude is that?

"Besides, the grand master gave you permission to receive offerings only for a period of three years. That time has already passed and yet you are still malingering here. Have you forgotten the agreement you made?"

Before he could complete his tirade the statue fell to the ground and was smashed to bits. The monks were incredulous. They waited until Scholar Zhou had left Suzhou and then raised funds to rebuild the statue.

The new Guanyin, however, was not able to perform the remarkable deeds of the previous statue.

# *Butterfingered Scholar Wu*

In May of 1760, during the reign of the Qianlong emperor, the head prefect of Feng County, Lu Shichang, set about revising the local gazetteer. He hired a scholar from Suzhou by the name of Wu as the project's chief scribe.

It was customary with these sorts of projects that all involved would live at the work site. So Wu left home to take up residence and employment in Feng County.

One morning, before work had begun for the day, Wu bowed deeply to his colleagues and said, "I will die soon and I am afraid that all the work I have started will be left to you."

His colleagues were puzzled at this strange declaration and asked how on earth he knew he was about to die.

He told them rather sadly, "On my way here I passed through Pei County, where I was approached by a woman who asked if she could share my carriage. I told her I was not in a position to invite her in because my carriage was already rather cramped.

"I continued on my way, and to my great surprise, each time I looked back at the road we had just traveled, this same woman was running along behind. She followed the carriage for more than twenty miles. When I asked the driver what he thought of this strange woman he didn't know which woman I meant. Then I knew she was a ghost.

"That night we stopped at an inn, and just as I was dozing off, the same woman appeared out of nowhere and sat on my bed.

"She said, 'Why don't we get married? We're both twenty-nine years old so it would be a perfect match.'

"I was absolutely stupefied by her presence as well as her suggestion, but all I could do was throw a pillow at her. She vanished in a flash, and although I saw nothing of her for the rest of the night, a voice demanding marriage whispered ceaselessly in my ear. She never used my name. Instead she called me by the name of a famous calligrapher.

"It seemed as if there would be no end to this annoyance, so I said to her, 'I'll give you anything if only you'll leave me in peace. What do you want?'

"She replied, 'I want two hundred cash put in the loft. Then I'll leave you.'

"I placed the money in the loft, but nothing changed—the money wasn't removed and her pestering continued unabated."

On hearing of this dreadful predicament, his friends were all terribly sympathetic. In a bid to protect Wu from the ghost, they allocated two boys to be his constant guards.

Several days later they heard a tremendous scream from the upstairs room. They rushed up and found Scholar Wu in a heap on the floor. A knife had been plunged into his abdomen and his intestines spilled out through the wound. His throat had also been cut, brutally severing his esophagus. His colleagues lifted him to a nearby bed. All the while, Wu assured them he was not in any pain.

When Prefect Lu arrived to examine his employee, Scholar Wu beckoned him nearer. Wu then wrote the character for "fate" in the air and the bemused prefect asked, "What do you mean? Whose fate?"

Wu then said in a weak, scratchy voice, "It was a fatal attraction. She came again and begged me to join her in the underworld so that we could be married. I asked her how I should kill myself and she handed me a knife, saying, 'Here, use this.' I grabbed the knife and plunged it deep into my stomach.

"I was groaning in pain, but when she saw my agony the woman massaged the wound and said, 'Your pain will stop now.' Sure enough, where she had massaged me I no longer felt any pain.

"I asked her again, 'What should I do next?'

"She then made a gesture as if she were cutting her own throat and said, 'Do as I have shown you.' So I slashed at my throat with the knife. But this only made her cross. She stamped her foot and said with a sigh, 'This is hopeless! All you're doing is causing yourself unnecessary pain.'

"She massaged my throat wound and once again the pain disappeared. Then she pointed to a spot on the right side of my throat and said, 'This is a better spot.'

"By this stage I was becoming quite queasy, and so I said, 'My hands are so shaky I just can't grip the knife. I've got butterfingers. I'm really too weak to do it properly. Can't you help me?'

"So the woman loosened her hair, and as it fell to her shoulders she lunged at me with the knife. This time my colleagues heard my screams of pain and came running up. As soon as she heard the footsteps she threw the knife aside and disappeared."

Prefect Lu was intrigued by this confession, but seeing that the man was still quite weak he refrained from questioning him further and hurriedly called a doctor. The doctor was able to reconstruct Wu's abdomen and throat, and although it was some time before he was able to eat and drink, he eventually recovered with the help of a course of medication and plenty of rest.

As for the ghost, she was never seen again.

# *The Patriarch of Fox Fairies*

A young woman who lived in a Dai village in Yancheng County was once bewitched by a demon. She eventually grew tired of the host of ineffectual magic charms she had tried, and decided the time had come to take personal action against the demon. So, she lodged a complaint with the god of the Guandi temple that lay to the north of the village. After she burned her letter the demon did indeed cease its harassment.

One night not long after this, everyone in her household had an identical dream. A god dressed in full battle array spoke to them. "I am General Zhou, a subordinate of the great god of war, Guandi. A few days ago one of your family requested help in exorcising a demon. This demon was in fact a fox fairy and I have already executed the beast.

"However, tomorrow all of the fox's friends are planning to take up arms against me to avenge its death. I will need your support in this battle. So, bring your drums and cymbals to the temple to spur me on."

The next morning, the family hurried to the temple, their numbers swelled by supportive neighbors. From somewhere in the air they could hear the thundering of horses' hooves and the clanking of armor. They took these battle sounds to be their cue.

The people in the crowd picked up their drums and cymbals and began to beat the rhythms of the war drums with all their might. Soon a black smoke filled the courtyard, and as it wafted into the village the sky began to rain fox corpses.

Several days later, the family dreamed that General Zhou returned. He said, "I have offended the Patriarch of the Foxes by slaughtering so many of his kind. The patriarch has lodged a complaint against me with the heavenly emperor, and the imperial police will soon be investigating the case.

"I hope I can depend on your support when I make my defense." Zhou then left details of the time and place of the hearing.

At the appointed time, the family gathered at the temple, taking care to hide along the corridors leading to the hall. They waited until nightfall and then the emperor himself arrived in a carriage, surrounded by various guards and attendants.

Behind the entourage came a white-haired person escorted by two guards bearing a placard upon which was written "The Fox Patriarch." The patriarch had strong, sharp teeth and white eyebrows.

Next the god of war came forward and welcomed them most respectfully to his temple.

The fox patriarch then took the lead saying, "There is no doubt the mischievous young fox deserved to die, but your subordinate has taken the matter too far. He has cruelly and ruthlessly killed scores of other innocent foxes. This is completely unforgivable."

The god of war nodded his head as if he agreed, and the horrified villagers hurried out of their hiding places and knelt before the assembled court. They pleaded on General Zhou's behalf for lenience.

A scholar among the kneeling crowd, also named Zhou, then cursed the patriarch. "Your hair may be white with age but you're still as cunning as ever. It is you who should be begging for forgiveness! Your subordinates spend all their time seducing innocent women and ultimately it is your responsibility! How can you be patriarch to such shameless creatures? You should be beheaded!"

Faced with this barrage of insults, the fox patriarch merely smiled and said in a calm and relaxed manner, "If humans commit adultery, what would be their punishment?"

Scholar Zhou replied, "They would be beaten."

The old fox replied, "Since adultery is not punishable by death, why did my underlings face death? Even if one considers that they committed adultery across species, this is only a crime of marginally increased severity, deserving exile at the worst. But what has happened? General Zhou has slaughtered not just one fox but scores of foxes! What sort of justice is that?"

Before Scholar Zhou had a chance to reply, the emperor's verdict was heard. "The emperor has decided that General Zhou's vigilance against evil was excessive and the punishments he administered were far too severe for the crimes committed. However, the court has taken into account that Zhou was acting unselfishly and was prompted by pleas for help from villagers who were suffering from the fox fairy's mischievousness. His punishment will be the loss of a year's salary and transfer to Haizhou District."

The relieved villagers shouted with joy and then bowed their heads with prayers of thanks to the wisdom of heaven before heading back to their homes.

*Guandi, God of War, and His Subordinates*

# *Swindled by the Earth God's Wife*

At the Huju Gate area there is a famous doctor by the name of Tu Qieru who happens to be a very good friend of mine. His daughter-in-law, Madam Wu, is the younger sister of a famous personage renowned for his filial piety and honor.

In 1776 Madam Wu dreamed she met up with a Mr. Li, a local conscript who was begging for alms. Mr. Li was carrying on his person a set of Buddhist scriptures that predicted the future, and one of the events it foretold was that the Huju Gate area would soon suffer a calamitous fire.

Mr. Li claimed to be collecting alms to finance an opera in honor of the gods in the hope of preventing this fire, but Madam Wu remained only half convinced by his story. It was true that the scriptures included detailed notes on names and places, but it still seemed rather an unlikely event.

While she was hesitating, an old woman in a yellow blouse and a crimson skirt appeared and said to her: "On the third of September a blaze will occur and your family will be the first affected. My numerical calculations suggest that you will not escape.

"What you need to do to prevent this calamity is to burn spirit money and make a few animal sacrifices. That should appease the gods and with luck will ensure no one is killed in the fire."

When Madam Wu woke from her dream she inquired about Conscript Li and discovered he had died many years before. She then asked if anyone knew of the woman with the yellow blouse, but to no avail.

She grew increasingly suspicious about the information given her in the dream, so she went to the local earth god's temple. She was both astonished and fearful to find that the idol representing the earth god's wife was identical to the woman in her dream.

When she consulted her neighbors about the coincidence, they were equally fearful and hurried off to organize an extraordinary show of devotion and respect to the temple. They put on dramatic performances, made special offerings, and raised several hundred taels of gold with which they bought supplies to continue the ritual.

When September drew near, the Tu family moved all their smaller household items to a relative's house. From the first of September they stopped cooking in the house and when the day of the third arrived there was quiet all around the neighborhood.

The day passed without a fire and in fact my good friend Mr. Tu is still quite safe today.

# *The Good Little Ghost*

In Jinling there was a young fellow by the name of Ge who loved drinking and acting tough. He was forever harassing and bullying other people.

Early one morning he and a group of friends went to Yuhuatai Park, where they chanced upon a partly rotted coffin. A piece of a red skirt was hanging through the rotted boards.

Ge's companions baited him, saying: "You're pretty good at heckling people, but would you dare bother that thing in the coffin?"

Ge laughed. "Why not?" He strode to the coffin and beckoned to it several times, saying, "That's a good little girl, come out and have some wine with me!"

Ge's friends were most impressed with his bravado and roared with laughter before going their separate ways.

As he made his way home that evening Ge was tailed by a black shadow that chittered eerily, "Your good little girl has come for some wine."

Ge knew that this must be the ghost from the rotted coffin and decided to keep the upper hand. He boldly greeted the shadow, saying, "Come along with me, my good little ghost."

He made his way toward a wineshop, went upstairs, and ordered a jug of wine for two. He then raised his cup and toasted the black shadow.

None of the tavern's patrons could see the shadow, so they assumed Ge was an idiot and gathered around to have a bit of a laugh.

After Ge and the shadow had drunk for a while, Ge took off his hat, placed it on the table, and said, "I'm just going downstairs to relieve myself. I'll be back in a moment."

The shadow nodded in reply.

Ge went downstairs and immediately rushed home.

The bartender later noticed that one of his guests had left without taking his hat and so he filched it. But that night he was possessed by a ghost. He spent the entire night muttering and mumbling and by daybreak he had finally hanged himself.

The wineshop keeper later said laughingly, "That ghost couldn't even distinguish between two entirely different people. She could only recognize the hat!

"That 'good little girl' was not so good after all!"

# *The Ghosts Who Pretended They Could Speak Mandarin*

The current superintendent of transport for Hedong, Wu Yuncong, was once a secretary for the Board of Punishment. One day a festival was being held on the street outside Wu's residence, and a maid took his young son to see the fun.

While they were out, the little boy needed to empty his bladder and did so on the side of the road. Instantly he began to cry, and he kept on crying even after he had been taken home by the worried maid.

Nobody in the house could understand why he was crying until later that night, when the young boy suddenly spoke in Mandarin: "What a rude little boy! How dare he urinate on my head! I'll make sure you all pay for this insult!"

The crying then continued unabated throughout the night.

The next morning the incensed and exhausted Mr. Wu wrote a complaint against this ghost addressed to the city god. He then took the letter to the city god's temple and burned it.

The letter contained words to the effect, "I am a southerner and my young son has unintentionally offended a Mandarin-speaking ghost. This ghost is extremely wild and totally unscrupulous. Can you please investigate this case for me and bring some relief to my son?"

That night the house was peaceful, but the following night the young boy was once again tormented by the ghost.

When he spoke, again in Mandarin, he said, "You are merely a low-level official. How dare you humiliate our Brother Number Four. We are all going to take our revenge unless you give us some wine."

Mr. Wu's wife was keen to avoid any further chaos, so she brought out the wine for the ghost and his companions, saying, "Please accept this wine. I don't want any more trouble! So please, just drink it and leave."

The problem was not to be resolved that simply, however. As soon as one ghost had drunk his fill, another would demand more wine. Demands came for meat, sausages, and snacks from the Yang family shop across the road to accompany the wine. The ghosts began to make all sorts of high-pitched screeches.

The noise was unbearable, so Mr. Wu rushed forward and slapped his son about the face shouting, "You vermin! You've changed your speech to Mandarin just to imitate the officials. You'll really regret it if you're trying to pull rank on me by speaking Mandarin!"

He began to beat his son, but still the boy spoke in Mandarin.

In desperation Mr. Wu filed another complaint to the city god: "That Mandarin-speaking ghost has come back and possessed my son. I beg of you, please punish him and banish him from my home."

That evening the boy's parents heard the sound of whipping and beating from his room.

The ghosts could be heard crying out above the thuds, "Please! No more! Don't beat us any more! We'll leave, we promise!"

From then on, Wu's son had no more trouble with ghosts.

# *The City God Gets Drunk*

A scholar by the name of Shen Fengyu from Hangzhou made his living as a secretary in the judiciary of Wukang County.

One day a memorandum demanding the capture of a pirate by the name of Shen Yufeng passed down through his office. One of the other secretaries in the office saw the opportunity for a joke and quickly reversed the characters for *Feng* and *Yu* with red pen. The message now demanded the capture of Shen Fengyu.

The mischievous secretary showed Shen Fengyu the document, saying, "They're coming to get you! They'll be here to arrest you any minute!"

Shen didn't see anything funny in this at all. He snatched the memorandum and burned it.

That night he dreamed he was arrested by the ghost police. They rushed into his room, tied him up, and locked him in the city god's temple.

The city god sat in his seat of honor and shouted down at Shen, "So you are that murderous pirate! The blood of many people is on your hands! You really are the lowest form of life!" He then instructed his officers to torture the prisoner.

Shen hastily protested that he was a scholar from Hangzhou and not a pirate, but this only made the city god more angry.

He barked back at Shen, "The Regulations of the Underworld demand that we support our fellow bureaucrats in the Human World. Whenever we receive a memorandum from above, we act on it.

"Today we received a document from Wukang County that clearly identified you as a pirate and called for your immediate arrest. How dare you deny your crimes!"

Shen continued his attempts at defense by explaining how his friend, Yuan, had played a stupid trick by reversing the names, but the city god refused to listen. The order was then given that Shen be beaten with thick cudgels as punishment.

As Shen screamed in pain from the beatings one of the officers leaned over and whispered to him, "The city god got drunk with his wife today, so if you want a fair hearing, you had better see another magistrate."

Shen glanced up at the city god. Sure enough, his face was bright red and his eyelids drooped from the effects of his drinking binge. There was no use pleading for mercy from this drunken city god, so Shen had no choice but to endure the beating.

Once this was over, the city god ordered that Shen be escorted to a nearby jail. On the way there, they passed by the temple of the god of war, Guandi.

Shen saw his chance and shouted as loudly as he could: "I have been unjustly punished!"

The god of war took up this complaint and called Shen over to explain his case.

After Shen had recounted the sequence of events, Guandi drew a piece of yellow paper from his desk and wrote out a lengthy ruling on the matter in red pen.

"It is clear from your manner of speech that you are indeed a scholar. The city god had no right to conduct a hearing and administer punishments while inebriated. I will see that he is punished for this crime.

"Moreover, your fellow secretary Mr. Yuan should not play around with other people's lives in such a flippant manner, so I will take away his own life as punishment.

"Finally, your immediate superior has been neglectful of his duties, allowing such folly to take place in his offices. But since he was away on business yesterday, I will only fine him three months' salary.

"As for you, Mr. Shen, your beating has irreparably damaged your intestines, and you'll certainly die as a result. However, I will arrange for your reincarnation. You will be reborn as the son of a Shanxi family.

"When you are only twenty years old you will pass the third level of the imperial examinations and become an official. This should recompense you for some of the grievances you have suffered in your current life."

This speech sent the ghost police scampering back to the Underworld.

When Shen woke from his dream, he felt a great pain in his stomach and called out to his colleagues for help. He told them of the dream, and sure enough, within three days he was dead.

When Yuan heard of Shen's death he was gripped with fear. He immediately resigned from his position as secretary and headed back to his hometown. Not long after this, however, he died vomiting blood.

Around the same time, the city god's statue fell from its base for no apparent reason, and Shen's superior, the magistrate, was fined three months' salary for misappropriation of government revenue.

*Scene from the Underworld*

## *Two Great Ways to Deal with Ghosts*

Luo Zhenren always tells people not to be afraid of ghosts. He advises that if you meet one, you should use a technique called "conquering the invisible with the invisible." This involves blowing at the ghost.

He maintains that ghosts are most terrified of human breath. This method is far better than slashing wildly with a knife or a stick, even though one may think a knife would be more effective.

Zhang Qishi is of the opinion that when you meet a ghost you should not be afraid. He argues that it is more important to fight it straightaway.

If you win the fight, then you're to be congratulated. If you lose, then the worst that can happen is that you'll become a ghost yourself.

# *The Immortal Prostitute*

Near Suzhou there is a mountain called Mount Xiqi, and behind this is a peak called Yun'ai. It is said that many immortals live on this peak, and rumor has it that those who climb the peak and survive automatically become immortals.

A certain scholar by the name of Wang had become depressed at his repeated failure at the national examinations, so he decided to climb Mount Yun'ai to try his luck as an immortal. He packed up some food and personal effects and said farewell to his family, then began his ascent.

When he reached the top he found a substantial plateau dotted with a few trees among the wispy clouds. His eyes caught sight of movement on a distant ridge, and when he peered across he could make out a woman walking among the trees. Thinking this a strange place to find a woman, he rushed over to take a closer look.

The woman was curious about this new arrival and approached him. As she drew nearer, Wang recognized her as the famous Suzhou prostitute Xie Chongniang, with whom he had fallen in love six or seven years earlier.

Seeing her old friend again, she was extremely pleased and immediately took his hand and led him back to a small thatched hut. It had no door and the floor was layered an inch deep in pine needles, making it quite soft and warm.

Chongniang then related the events that had passed since they last met.

"After we parted, I was put under arrest by Prefect Wang. He stripped me naked and beat me ruthlessly, until the flesh on my buttocks was torn to shreds. Besides the pain, I felt most keenly the humiliation of the punishment. I was a high-ranking prostitute who commanded quite a bit of respect within the industry. How could I face anyone after such a humiliation?

"So I devised a plan to leave. I told the brothel owner that I was going to a temple to make some offerings, but instead I intended to commit suicide by jumping off a nearby cliff. I did jump, but instead of falling to my death I became entangled in the vines and creepers that grew along the cliff face.

"I had been hanging there for a while when an old woman with long white hair came to my rescue. She freed me from the vines, nourished me with pine nuts, and taught me how to concentrate my energies.

"Eventually, I felt neither hunger nor cold, and although I was a little scared at first, after a year of braving the elements I lost all my fear.

"The old woman lives just over on the next mountain, and she came by here yesterday to tell me that I would meet an old lover today. That's why I was wandering around on the plateau. I never dreamed it would be you!"

She paused and then asked, "Is Prefect Wang dead?"

He replied, "I have no idea, but now that you're an immortal you wouldn't be harboring thoughts of revenge, would you?"

The woman replied, "If it wasn't for Prefect Wang, I wouldn't be where I am today. I suppose I should be thankful and not vengeful.

"The old woman told me once that on one of her trips to heaven she had seen Prefect Wang being whipped by a god. The prefect was recounting his sins as he faced each crack of the whip. I figured he must be dead if he was seen in heaven."

The scholar declared, "Wang has no business beating prostitutes!"

The woman replied, "Those who aren't moved by beautiful women and sex, despite their love for them, are true sages. Those who are moved by beautiful women and sex are human, and those who know nothing of beauty and sex and are unmoved by them are beasts. Heaven hates this type most of all.

"When Prefect Wang beat me he was showing off to his direct superior, Governor Xu Shilin. Xu was known as a conservative neo-Confucian, and Wang wanted to make an example of me to ingratiate himself with Xu. Heaven hates that type of behavior most of all. Besides, Wang has committed many other crimes against heaven."

The scholar then asked, "Immortals are supposed to be pure, yet you spent your life as a prostitute. How did you manage to become an immortal with that sort of past?"

She replied, "Although sex is not an act of propriety, love between men and women is the essence of the universe. If a butcher lays down his knife, then he can become a Buddha in that instant. Prostitution is no more sinful than a whole range of other human practices."

He then told her his own plans to become an immortal and asked if he could stay in her hut while he learned.

"You are most welcome to stay with me, but I fear that the path to immortality is not an easy one for you," she said.

They arranged some bedding on the pine-needle floor, removed their clothing, and lay together as they had before. There was a major difference, however. She never said anything romantic or intimate, and although he was free to touch her smooth, white buttocks, if he became aroused she would become very solemn and tigers and other wild mountain beasts would howl outside the hut. Some would even poke their heads in and scratch at the walls. It was as if they were overseeing the reunion.

This went on for some time, until all the scholar could do was lie quietly with his arms around the prostitute.

Once, in the middle of the night, he heard people milling around and carriages bustling past, just outside the hut. He was quite puzzled at such a commotion on an isolated mountain peak.

"That is just the mountain gods coming and going. They like to visit each other at night, and as long as I don't interfere they don't bother me," the woman explained.

At dawn, she broke the news that he would have to leave.

"Your friends and relatives are waiting for you at the base of the mountain. Hurry now, go back to them," she said.

He refused to go, so she said, "The resolution of our fate will have to wait until the next time we meet." She led him to the edge of a cliff and pushed him off.

When he looked up from the foot of the precipice he saw the woman gazing longingly down at him. She stood there for a long while, then disappeared.

The scholar staggered down the road to his village and it wasn't long before he met his family, led by his elder brother, coming toward him. They were sobbing as they walked up the mountain.

It turned out that he had been dead for twenty-seven days. His family members were on their way to make offerings to the gods to protect him in the underworld.

After he had sufficiently recovered, the scholar went to the prefect's office to inquire about Prefect Wang. Sure enough, the prefect had died of a stroke some time ago.

# *Zhang Youhua*

A student from Anqing by the name of Chen Shuning lived in a dormitory in Huaining. On the Double Ninth Festival, when all the locals celebrate by climbing the nearby mountain, Chen went out for a stroll on his own. His wanderings took him out the south gate of the town and past a graveyard.

He noticed a pillar of black smoke coming from somewhere in the cemetery. His curiosity aroused, he wandered in among the tombs. Suddenly he felt a chill wind blow up. With his hair standing on end from both fear and cold, he hurried on his way.

At sleep that night, back in the supposed safety of his dormitory, he dreamed he was walking in a monastery. Everything was quite clean and serene. A mural painted on the eastern wall depicted a river flanked by pines.

The poem above the painting was titled "The Peony" and the first line read: "When the east wind blows, a streak of red will appear." Alongside the poem was the signature Zhang Youhua.

Chen was pondering the meaning of such a beautiful and cryptic line when a man pushed open a nearby door and entered the dormitory room. The man, who seemed to be about forty, was short with a red nose and piercing eyes.

He then addressed young Chen, saying, "I am Zhang Youhua and the poem you are reading was written by me. Do you sneer at my talent?"

Chen hastily replied, "Oh no, not at all! I would never presume to sneer."

Chen tried to explain himself but his words became thoroughly tangled.

The red-nosed man pointed straight at him and demanded: "Tell me, am I a man or a ghost?"

"I felt a chill wind when you came in, so I would say you are a ghost," Chen replied.

"Do you think I am a good ghost or a bad ghost?"

"Since you can write poetry I think you must be a good ghost," Chen said.

The red-nosed ghost rushed forward and grabbed at Chen, shouting: "Well, you're wrong! I am a very evil ghost!"

As he came closer, the air around Chen became colder and colder. The chill went right through Chen's insides and it felt just as if his heart had been frozen in ice. Chen ran to cover behind a bamboo bedframe, but the ghost merely reached through and grabbed him by the testicles. The pain was excruciating and Chen woke from his nightmare with a start.

When he looked at his testes, he saw to his horror that they were swollen to an enormous size. From then on he suffered from consecutive bouts of raging fever and severe chills. The doctor who was called in could do nothing to ease the pain, and it wasn't long before Chen died, right there in the student dormitory.

The prefect of Huaining arranged for his funeral and pondered the needless death of his young friend. One day the prefect happened to run into a retired official. He asked the man, "Do you know if there was anyone by the name of Zhang Youhua who used to live around here?"

He was told, "Yes, I do. A clerk who worked here in Anqing went by that name. He died about two years ago, but when he was alive he was a real troublemaker.

"He had a passion for writing poetry but his verse was always rather odd. He was rather short and had a bright red nose, if I remember correctly. They buried him out by the south gate."

It was clear to all that this was the very place where Chen had encountered the chill wind while taking his walk.

# *A Ghost Borrows an Official Title for a Daughter's Marriage*

In Xinjian there was a scholar by the name of Zhang Yacheng who from the time he was a child loved to make his own toys and costumes. His attic was filled with helmets, beautiful dresses, and a variety of precious bits of shiny patterned paper. He would play with his treasures by himself in the attic, and as an adult he kept his toys. But their existence remained a secret from his family.

One day he opened the door to a woman of about thirty who asked Zhang if he would make her several items of clothing and numerous pieces of jewelry. She offered to pay, so Zhang agreed. He then inquired as to her plans for the garments and jewelry.

"I'll be using these as my wedding clothes," she replied.

Zhang was sure she was pulling his leg, but he didn't think it worth persisting with the question so he let it rest.

The next day the woman returned and told him, "You have a neighbor of official rank by the name of Tang. My husband's surname is also Tang and I would like him to have the same rank as your neighbor.

"Could you write down his name and title for me? Put the surname at the top in the position of honor, if you wouldn't mind."

Zhang was sure she was joking, but it seemed a harmless enough request, so he took a piece of paper and wrote down the name and title for her.

The next evening, just after Zhang had prepared the package of clothing and jewelry, the woman arrived with cakes and money to thank him for his trouble. But the next morning, when Zhang looked more closely at the gifts, he saw that the cakes were made of mud and the cash was ghost money. It was then that he realized the woman was a ghost.

Several days later the mountains around the village were lit up with lights and filled with music. The puzzled villagers gathered outside their houses to watch, and they concluded the commotion must be a funeral being held among the existing graves.

As they approached the scene of the noise, they realized it was not a funeral at all. Instead it was a wedding—all the distant figures had red wedding flowers in their lapels.

The villagers knew that nobody lived among the graves, so a few of the village busybodies went closer to the festivities to investigate. They saw the area festooned with lanterns upon which the character for *Tang* and an official rank were painted.

When the villagers heard this, they came to the realization that ghosts also love to put on vain shows of wealth and rank to impress their friends.

Indeed, ghosts and people are identical in this regard.

# *The Bear*

A merchant from Zhejiang Province frequently made sea journeys for business purposes. On one of these journeys, he and his twenty or so employees were blown off course and onto an island. Since they were there, the men decided to explore the new territory.

They had walked only about a mile when they came across what they later described as a bear. It was over ten feet tall and extremely strong. By hitting the men with its giant paws, the bear herded them into a tight group under a tree. It then tied the men to the tree and to each other by threading a vine through holes it pierced in their ear lobes. Having completed this task to its satisfaction, the bear skipped gleefully away.

The men waited until they thought the bear was far enough away and then drew their knives, cut the vine, and ran back to the boat. Not long after this, they saw four bears walking along the shore carrying a stone platform on top of which sat a bear of enormous proportions. The bear that had tied them up led the party towards the tree, skipping all the way. When it reached the base of the tree and saw the vine slashed, the bear looked confused and very disappointed. The bear on the platform, however, was clearly enraged. It then gave what must have been an order for the four other bears to punish the first bear. The beating was so severe that the bear was killed.

The men on the boat, watching from the distance, were terrified at the brutality of what they had just witnessed. All the same they were relieved to have escaped with their own lives. One of the men who had his ears pierced during this adventure was a Mr. Wu of Shanyin. A relative, Shen Pingru, asked Wu how he had come to have pierced ears and this was the story Wu told.

# *Two Corpses Make Love in the Wilderness*

There once lived a brave old itinerant who spent his time wandering alone around Hunan and Guangdong. He did, however, regularly return to an old deserted temple. One bright moonlit night he decided to go for an evening stroll in the nearby forest.

In the distance he saw a figure dressed in the clothes of the Tang dynasty. Deducing he had chanced upon a ghost, our fearless itinerant followed the figure through the thick undergrowth and watched as it descended into an ancient grave.

The itinerant decided this must be one of the "rigor-mortis corpses," who forfeit all their power if they lose the lid of their coffin. Resolving to steal the lid, he resumed his place in the undergrowth the following night and waited for the corpse to leave.

Around the second watch, the corpse indeed left the grave. It appeared to be heading in the direction our brave itinerant had seen it coming from the previous night. Curiosity aroused, the man followed the ghost to a huge mansion.

The ghost stood beneath an open window inside which stood a woman dressed in red. She threw down a long, white scarf and the corpse quickly climbed up into her room. Thereafter the man could hear a lot of noise, but gradually all was quiet. He decided to return alone to the now vacant grave to hide the coffin lid. Having done so, he concealed himself in some thick bushes in the nearby pine forest.

Just before dawn the corpse came hurrying back to the grave. When he saw his coffin lid was missing he flew into a panic and ran about, searching high and low. He finally gave up and hurried back to the mansion, with the itinerant following. Once there the corpse leaped about screaming wildly, trying to attract the attention of the woman inside.

When she finally appeared, she waved at him as if to tell him to leave. When he refused, she looked very shocked indeed. Then the cocks crowed, heralding the start of a new day. In that instant the corpse fell to the roadside in a heap.

That day a crowd of shocked people gathered to see the corpse. When they reached the mansion, it was discovered the building was actually an ancestral temple for the Zhou family. On venturing inside they discovered in an upstairs room the corpse of a woman lying next to an empty coffin. It was then everyone realized that these two corpses must have been copulating in the wilderness each night.

They then decided to cremate the corpses together.

# *King Buffalo Head*

Zhuang Guangyu of Liyang Village dreamed one night that a monster with horns protruding from its gruesome head came knocking at his door.

The monster said to Zhuang, "I am King Buffalo Head and the Great Lord on High has instructed me to come here and receive offerings. If you build a statue in my likeness, I will ensure prosperity and good fortune."

The next morning Zhuang told his fellow villagers of the strange dream. They were extremely enthusiastic about the prospect of good fortune, as the village was currently in the midst of an epidemic.

"It would pay us to trust in this monster. Besides, we've nothing to lose." They rallied around and pooled their savings, reaching a grand total of several tens of thousands. With the proceeds they built three thatched huts and a statue in the image of King Buffalo Head. The statue was duly positioned in the middle hut and from hereon in, the villagers made regular offerings to the king.

It wasn't long before the epidemic disappeared. Even more convincing, those folk who asked to give birth to sons appeared to have their wishes granted. The temple, needless to say, became the focus for generous offerings and incense for several years to follow.

Then one day, a villager by the name of Zhou Manzi went to the temple to seek a cure for his young son's smallpox. He made generous offerings of freshly killed meat as part of his worship, and his horoscope was read while he was there so he would have some indication of his son's fate. The horoscope predicted a positive outcome for his son's future. Zhou was ecstatic, so he hired a troop of actors to perform outside the temple as an expression of his gratitude.

A few days later, however, Zhou's son was dead. This turn of events left Zhou furious.

"I was relying on my son to till the fields and feed me in my old age.

It would have been better if I had died in his place!"

In a fit of rage, he and his wife took up their garden hoes, stormed into the temple, and smashed the statue. They began with the head and continued until the temple itself was reduced to a pile of rubble.

The rest of the villagers were terrified. They were certain a great calamity would befall the village as a consequence of this vandalism. In actual fact nothing untoward happened in the village, and to this day nobody knows where the god with the buffalo head went.

# *The Muddleheaded Ghost*

In 1774, during the reign of the Qianlong emperor, a young rascal by the name of Hanliu was detained in the capital on charges of beating and injuring his father. The Board of Punishment investigated the case and it was decided that Hanliu should be executed.

One of deputies of the board, however, was of the opinion that since the attack had not been fatal, the death sentence was not appropriate. He was overruled by the chief justice, Mr. Qin, who personally wrote a memorial to the throne arguing that the relationship between father and son was sacred and Hanliu had committed a grave sin by injuring his father.

The throne upheld the death penalty and furthermore sent the Board of Punishment's secretary, Mr. Li Huaizhong, to supervise the execution.

Three days after the execution Hanliu's ghost possessed Secretary Li and said, "All the other officials were prepared to forgive me but you insisted on having me executed. I have carried this grievance to the grave and now, as a ghost, I have resolved to take your life."

Everyone who heard this ranting was shocked at the ghost's muddleheaded understanding of the debate surrounding his execution, but they were completely powerless. Li was bedridden from that day on, and it wasn't long before he had passed away.

# *The Ghost That Stood in Awe of the Powerful*

A young man by the name of Zhang Balang had an affair with one of his maids, but as soon as he was married he abandoned her. This maid fell into a deep depression and soon died of misery.

"I will never forgive Balang for the way he has treated me!" she said with her dying breath.

Then all of a sudden her eyes popped open again and she said, "Balang carries an extremely strong karma, so it will be difficult to exact my revenge on him personally. I think I'll go for his wife instead!"

Before two years were up, Balang's wife had died from complications during childbirth.

# *The Lovesick Ghost*

In Yuezhou there is a man from the Zhang family with the name Third Master Ghost. The name arose from the fact that he was the third son born, but also because his father was a ghost. His nominal father was a scholar at an academy, and his mother, a Madam Chen, was an incredibly sensual woman.

One day, as Scholar Zhang and his wife lay resting on their bed, a ghost who called himself Little God Yunyang appeared out of nowhere and started having intercourse with Madam Chen.

Zhang felt himself pushed aside and from then on he was unable to do anything at all. It was as if his hands and feet were bound fast.

After this episode the Zhangs bought various charms and amulets in an attempt to expurgate the demon, but none of these had any effect. The ghost continued to visit Madam Chen. She became pregnant three months later and gave birth to a boy.

On the day of the birth strange, ghostly noises filled the air. It appeared the ghosts had come to offer their congratulations, for lots of coins dropped from the sky.

Mr. Zhang was extremely angry about the whole affair and went to Mount Longhu to ask a resident Daoist priest for help.

One morning after this, Little God Yunyang came staggering into Madam Chen's bedroom dripping with sweat, saying, "I'm in deep trouble. Last night I went to your neighbor Mr. Mao's place and stole his golden vase. Unfortunately, Zhong Kui, a figure in one of the scrolls hanging on the wall, leaped out of the picture and chased me, swords and all.

"I was absolutely terrified that he would do some real damage, so I ran off and threw the vase into the pond by the West Lane. I've come here to seek your help! Please give me some alcohol to calm my nerves."

Madam Chen told her husband what had happened and Zhang went to confirm the story with the Mao family.

It turned out they really had lost their golden vase the previous night. The entire household was in turmoil and they were just about to report the incident to the police in the hope of apprehending the thief.

Zhang then interceded. "I can help you retrieve your vase, but I would like something in return."

Mr. Mao was ecstatic and said, "You can choose whatever you like, if only you find my golden vase for me."

Zhang pretended to go into a trance by chanting an incantation, and after quite some time told everyone to go to the pond by the West Lane. The good swimmers among them were ordered to dive in and search the bottom for the vase. Sure enough, the vase was found.

Mr. Mao asked Scholar Zhang to take the seat of honor at their table and asked what Zhang would like in return.

"Well, a scholar like me isn't really concerned about money or material possessions, but I really would like a book or a couple of scrolls from your collection. One or two pieces would be plenty," Zhang said.

So the Mao family showed Zhang their collection and he chose a painting of a hibiscus by Wen Zhengming. The Maos insisted that this alone was far too little and that unless he chose another piece they would really feel very badly.

Zhang pointed at the scroll of Zhong Kui hanging on the wall and said, "Can I take this one as my second scroll? Would that be all right?"

Mr. Mao reluctantly agreed to this request and Zhang returned home with the scroll and immediately hung it on the wall.

From that day on, Little God Yunyang never invaded their bedroom again. However, a ghost could be heard crying and wailing in the trees of the courtyard for three whole days after the scroll was hung. Everyone said that the ghost was lovesick.

# *Thunder Strikes the Earth God*

During the reign of the Kangxi emperor, the prefect of Shidai was a man by the name of Wang Yixin. He was a very close friend of a man called Lin. After his death Lin became the earth god for Shidai, and the two friends, though separated by death, would get together every evening and chat late into the night, just as they had before.

On one of these occasions the earth god whispered secretively to Wang, "Your family faces a great calamity. I had to tell you. Though I'm pretty sure I'll be punished by the Powers That Be for leaking confidential information."

Wang begged for details of the nature of this calamity and finally he was told, "Your mother will be struck by lightning."

Wang was flabbergasted and pleaded with his friend to help prevent this misfortune. Wang received the reply:

"This is a debt of karma that your mother has accumulated during her previous lives. Besides, how can I help when my rank is so low?"

Wang begged and pleaded tearfully for any idea that might prevent this calamity.

Eventually the earth god acquiesced. "There is one possibility. You must behave in the most filial manner possible. You should also increase your mother's belongings and food ten times. That includes everything she wears, eats, and drinks as part of her normal daily life.

"If you do this, she will consume her allocation of life's luxuries in a minimum period and will thus reach the point of death more quickly. If she dies in this way, she will go peacefully. The thunder god won't be able to do anything to her," the earth god assured him.

Wang did as his friend advised, and surely enough his mother died within a few years.

Three years after her death there was a torrential downpour, and in a flash the thunder god appeared right inside Wang's house. He paced aggressively around the coffin containing the body of Wang's mother, and suddenly the room was filled with a tremendous noise, flashes of light, and the pungent odor of sulfur.

The thunder god, unable to strike his desired target, had split the house open in revenge. Then the lightning forked out towards the earth god's temple, struck the statue, and reduced it to mud.

# *Zhang Guangxiong*

In Zhili there was an intelligent, good-looking young man by the name of Zhang Guangxiong. When he reached the age of eighteen, he moved into the western chambers of his family home to study in quieter surroundings. In the house of a wealthy family there were always plenty of maidservants around, but Zhang's parents kept him closely supervised to ensure that nothing untoward happened between their son and the maids.

On the night of the seventh of July, when the town celebrated the festival of lovers, Zhang Guangxiong sat in his study dreaming of the legendary romance between the cowherd and the weaving maid. As he gazed at the stars he began to think that he would rather fancy it if one of the maids accompanied him while he studied.

In the midst of this fantasy, a beautiful woman suddenly appeared outside his window. He called out to her but received no reply. Only a short time later, though, she came strolling into his room and stopped directly in front of him. He looked carefully at her and soon realized she was not one of the maids employed in the house, so he asked her name.

"I am Miss Wang," she said.

He then persisted with his questioning. "Do you live around here?"

"I live to the west of your house, so we are in fact neighbors. I have long been an admirer of yours, so today I decided to come and meet you in person," she replied.

Zhang was ecstatic and it wasn't long before they were back in his bedroom making love. She came every night after this to sleep with Zhang.

Zhang had always had a houseboy sleeping in his room with him, but Miss Wang objected to his presence. "We don't need your little slave so nearby now. Why don't you send him further away? If we need him, we can always call him."

Zhang told the boy to sleep in an outer room, but the boy refused, saying, "I figured there was something going on when I heard all those noises of love-making coming from your bed. But your father ordered me to protect and serve you, so I dare not leave."

Zhang was at a loss, and he told Miss Wang when she returned that night.

"Don't worry about it. I'll fix him. He's really in trouble this time," she said.

That night, just as the houseboy was dozing off, he was grabbed by a monster, dragged outside to the western garden, and strung up in a tree. He called out to his master for help but the only response he received was from Miss Wang.

"I'll let you go on the condition that you leave us alone. You'll have to sleep in the outside rooms. Be warned, if you tell anyone about this, especially the old master, then I'll really make you suffer."

The terrified houseboy agreed to her terms and was forthwith lowered to the ground.

The couple lived secretly for over a year, during which time young Zhang became more and more emaciated. Zhang's father, noting the dramatic change in his son, interrogated the houseboy, but was told there was nothing amiss in their chambers. The elder Zhang felt that there was something suspicious about the houseboy's manner—he seemed somewhat embarrassed and depressed—so he decided to go and check out his son's activities for himself.

That night he crept into Zhang's chambers and heard a woman's voice coming from the bedroom. He immediately kicked in the partition and stormed into the room, but when he raised the bed curtains there was nobody to be seen except young Zhang himself.

After a brief search he found a gold hairpin under the pillow and the petals of a wild tea-flower. He knew then and there that his son must be consorting with a demon, because there were no tea-flowers in this region. Angered and disappointed he whipped his son mercilessly.

Zhang was in no position, after this, to explain to his father, and at any rate his father had arranged for a famous Daoist priest to come and exorcise the spirit. The priest built a small altar and began his ritual chanting.

That night Zhang was visited by Miss Wang again, but this time she was in tears.

"Our secret is out so I must say goodbye," she said.

Zhang was grief-stricken at this news and just before she left he asked, "Will we ever meet again?"

"I'll meet you in Huazhou, twenty years from now," she replied. Then she disappeared.

After this, Zhang's life continued upon a more regular path—he married a Miss Chen, passed the provincial level examinations, and was appointed a prefect in Wujiang. Eventually he was promoted to the position of magistrate in Huazhou, and it was not long after this transfer that his wife died.

*Daoist Exorcist*

His father arranged a second marriage for his widower son, but this time to a girl from the Wang family. The bride traveled to Huazhou for the wedding, and when Zhang finally saw his new wife face to face on their wedding night he realized that her features were identical to those of Miss Wang, who had visited him in his study those nights so long ago.

Puzzled at the coincidence, he asked his wife her age and was told that she was just twenty.

It then dawned on him, "That fox fairy must have been deeply in love with me. She's been reincarnated as my new wife."

When he asked the bride about their previous encounters she was completely confused—she had no recollection of them at all.

# *The Blue-Capped Demon*

In Yangzhou, a merchant by the name of Wang Chunshan had a troupe of professional actors in his permanent employ. One member of this troupe was a Suzhou man, Zhu Erguan, who was not only a talented actor but also extremely handsome. Wang decided to reward this outstanding talent and arranged for Zhu to live in a private garden outside the Xuning Gate.

One day the house neighboring the garden caught on fire, and before long the blaze had spread to Zhu's garden. Zhu fled for his life to the lane outside. On the western side of this lane, Zhu saw two lovely women leaning against a doorway waving to him. He approached them and asked if he could take shelter in their house.

The two beauties explained to Zhu that they were distant cousins of the Wang clan, and were thus related to Wang Chunshan.

The three were just getting acquainted when suddenly a man about fifty years old walked in and declared that he was the father of the two women. He was dressed in a leopard-fur coat and wore a blue cap. Confronted with his daughters in such a compromising position, he insisted that Zhu set things right and marry the girls.

While it was true that Zhu did rather fancy the two beauties, he was in no position to marry them. He came from a poor family that had no possibility of finding the necessary betrothal gifts.

He told the man in the blue cap of his plight and received the brusque reply: "Don't worry about it. I'll cover the costs."

Zhu then requested permission to return to his parents in Suzhou to tell them his plans.

The man in the blue cap replied: "By all means tell your parents, but don't let them worry about money or status. My daughters place great value in your looks.

"I have one request, though. Don't mention your marriage to my nephew, Wang Chunshan."

Zhu promptly took the next boat home to break the good news to his father.

His father, a poor carpenter, pleaded with him to forget the match. There was no way a poor carpenter could pay for such a wedding.

Zhu returned to tell the blue-capped man about his father's fears, and in reply was given two thousand coins by his future father-in-law to defray the wedding costs. The coins were stamped as Kangxi currency and were strung together with red ribbon.

Clutching his treasure, Zhu began the journey home. Unfortunately, he was spotted with the money by a couple of the local magistrate's men. These gentlemen of the law arrested him immediately. "Money fitting this description has just been reported stolen from the cashbox of one of the local gentry families. You are in possession of stolen property and we arrest you on suspicion of theft," they said.

Zhu was taken back to the magistry for questioning and promptly told the magistrate about the blue-capped man and his own forthcoming marriage.

Locals who had gathered to hear the case found the story unbelievable, so the magistrate stated, "If you can show us this mysterious blue-capped person, you can go free."

Zhu was greatly relieved and explained, "My fianceés' father gave me the money with instructions to prepare the wedding for today, so the bridal sedan should be along soon. Wait and see."

Surely enough, it wasn't long before the sound of drums could be heard, and gradually the waiting townsfolk could hear a wedding procession approaching. Four people wearing red short-sleeved shirts bore the bridal sedan.

The townsfolk rushed over and lifted the curtain of the chair, and there in place of the beautiful brides sat a green-faced monster with long teeth. Of course everyone was terrified by this sight and they all fled the scene—including the officers responsible for Zhu's arrest.

Zhu was thus able to escape conviction. He returned home only to find in his sitting room the man in the blue cap.

The latter promptly set about abusing Zhu. "You were sworn to secrecy over this wedding and yet look what you've done.

"Not only did you tell absolutely everyone about me but worse still you've got the law onto me. What sort of gratitude is that?"

He then shouted to his attending manservants and instructed them to beat Zhu as punishment for his breach of trust.

On hearing of this crisis, the daughters begged their father to show mercy and forgive Zhu.

Faced with his daughters' entreaties, the blue-capped man relented and the marriage ceremony continued.

After they'd been married a month, the new brides and the bridegroom returned to Yangzhou to see the girls' father.

After more than a year of marital bliss the two women prepared a surprise banquet for Zhu during which they broke the news of their impending departure.

"Our time as earthly beings is drawing to a close. Fate dictates that we can no longer be with you. You must return to your hometown."

Zhu was distraught and sobbed that he would never leave them. And so it went for a couple of days—the wives crying and pleading with him to leave, and Zhu in his misery refusing.

Then came the sudden arrival of the blue-capped man. He insisted Zhu leave, but the troubled young actor clung to his brides and refused to let go.

At this show of resistance, the blue-capped man grew angry. He pushed Zhu across the room and then threw him up into the air. Zhu hit the ground heavily and immediately lost consciousness.

When he woke and looked around he found to his surprise that he had been thrown up to the foothills of Mount Huqiu—near his old hometown.

## *Cousin Raccoon*

One of the lanes in Liuhe County, Laomei Lane, is renowned for raccoon sightings. Some nights these strange raccoons wander round the houses calling through the windows: "Cousin, oh Cousin!" in an attempt to bewitch the unwary. If they hear no replies they usually just wander off again.

One night, however, a young man of the Xia family was studying alone in a temple when he heard someone calling his name. He carelessly opened the window and looked out into the moonlight to see who was looking for him.

There in the street stood an extremely coarse and ugly woman. Xia was just about to tell her to leave him in peace when she rushed through the window, forced him into a bedroom, and ripped off his pants. She then sucked on his penis until all his semen had been extracted.

It is said these raccoons are immensely powerful creatures and people don't stand a chance against them. They are also said to be extremely smelly, and wherever their paws have been the odor lingers for over a month.

# *An Imprisoned Ghost*

In Shangyu County there was a magistrate by the name of Xing who had terrible marital problems. One day, while he and his wife were in the midst of a quarrel, Xing slapped her. In a fury, the wife hanged herself. Three days after her death she became a ghost and began haunting her old home.

Whenever Xing got into bed with his concubine, a chill wind blew up, rustling the bed curtains and sometimes even blowing out the candle. Xing was furious at this harassment, so he called in a Daoist monk to exorcise the ghost.

The monk performed the necessary rituals and once he had succeeded in capturing the ghost he sealed it in a chamber on the eastern side of the house.

Placing some magic charms as well as an official seal on the door, the Daoist assured Xing that the ghost would not escape. Indeed, Xing experienced no further trouble from his wife's ghost.

After a while, Xing was transferred to Qiantang County. His replacement at the Shangyu magistry was, naturally, unfamiliar with the previous occupants' problems, and he opened up the eastern chamber, unwittingly releasing the ghost. The newly freed ghost then possessed a young maid and the turmoil and chaos in the Shangyu magistry began all over again.

The new magistrate confronted the ghost directly, saying, "Your fight is with Mr. Xing and has nothing to do with my maid. Why do you want to harm her?"

"Actually, I don't want to harm her. I merely planned to use her body as a medium through which I could seek your help," the ghost replied.

The magistrate then asked how he could be of assistance.

"I want you to send me to Xing's new place at Qiantang," the ghost explained.

The magistrate was a bit puzzled. "What's stopping you from going there yourself?"

"Because I am the ghost of a person who died wrongfully, I will fail the Underworld's immigration inspections unless I have an official pass with the official seal," she said.

She would need two officers from the magistry to accompany her as well as this pass. When the magistrate asked which two officers she wanted, she named two deceased men who had previously worked at the magistry, Chen Gui and Teng Sheng.

The magistrate complied with all of her requests. He wrote out an official statement granting her permission to travel and then burned it so that it would reach the appropriate ghost bureaucrats.

One day in distant Qiantang, the unsuspecting Xing was having a quiet dinner in his rooms when his concubine suddenly fell to the floor,

*Ghost King and Magistrate from the Underworld*

ranting, "You are totally shameless! After forcing me to my death you then inflict upon me starvation and loneliness by imprisoning me in the eastern chamber.

"Now, I have returned to take my revenge on you, and you can be sure that I won't rest until I do!"

From then on, day and night, the Qiantang magistry was in complete chaos. Xing finally reached the end of his tether and called in another Daoist to exorcise the ghost a second time. The rituals were again successful and the ghost was captured and locked with various charms and seals in the Qiantang prison.

As the ghost was being carried into the prison, she screamed, "You really are completely heartless, aren't you? At least I was locked up in a room last time. Now I am being put in jail. What crime have I committed to deserve such treatment? I'll get my revenge, just see if I don't!"

A month later a very important criminal hanged himself in Xing's jail. Xing was stripped of his title and officially dismissed from the civil service for this failure of duty. This turn of events left Xing terrified. He vowed to shave his head and become a Buddhist monk, and some of his friends donated money so that he could perform the necessary rituals to join the order and officially become a monk.

Unfortunately, before all this could be arranged, Xing became extremely sick, and soon he was dead.

# *A Fox Fairy and a Ghost Invade the Stomach*

An imperial guard, Li Hongfeng, had a son by the name of Li Yi, who also had the official name Yi Shan, because he had once been a scholar in the Hanlin Academy.

Li Yi was a well-rounded scholar. He was able to expound knowledgeably on neo-Confucian philosophy, and he wrote excellent poetry and prose.

One evening while he was reading under the lamplight, two beautiful women appeared before him. They teased him mercilessly and soon grew quite brazen, and eventually Li found himself subjected to all sorts of lewd advances. With firm resolve Li remained impassive throughout the ordeal.

Later that evening, after Li had finished dinner, he heard a voice coming from his stomach. "I attached myself to some of the eggplants you ate for dinner. Now that I'm actually housed in your stomach, you won't be able to ignore me, will you?"

The voice was clearly that of one of the women who had attempted to seduce him under the lamplight earlier that evening.

From this day on, Li walked around with glazed eyes as if in some sort of trance. His behavior became more and more irregular. Sometimes, for no apparent reason, he would suddenly slap himself in the face. He was once seen out in a rainstorm kneeling on the ground with only a small pebble on his head for protection, making absolutely no effort to seek shelter from the torrent. Other times he would suddenly bow down before someone, placing his head on the floor in a mock form of worship, maintaining the position even while he was dragged away.

As the days passed his face grew sallow and pasty and his body grew thinner. It seemed that he would soon waste away. When the spirit wanted to communicate with others, Li acted as the medium and would variously write or speak the spirit's message.

One day a school friend of Li's, a man by the name of Jiang Shiquan, came and challenged the spirit directly, saying, "What on earth is a ravishingly beautiful thing like you doing with old Li? Why don't you come and try your luck with me?"

Li wrote the spirit's brief reply in two characters, which had the general meaning that they were not fated to be together.

Jiang tried again, asking, "Why would someone of your outstanding beauty want to live in such a disgusting place as Li's stomach?"

Li wrote the spirit's reply. "You really are too revolting. Go away!"

At the time, Li's father was fortunate enough to be on friendly terms with the governor of Jiangxi, a Mr. Wu.

Governor Wu, hearing of the Li family's predicament, invited the young scholar to his residence for a meeting with the Daoist grand master Zhang.

Zhang built an altar at the Tenghua Pavilion and commenced the purification of scholar Li—for three days they ate sacred vegetarian meals and chanted incantations. Grand Master Zhang's magicians then lifted a placard on which was written "We will exorcise the demon on the fifteenth of March."

When the day arrived, spectators had gathered from far and wide to view the exorcism. The grand master took a position at the center with the magicians seated along the sides. Li was asked to kneel before the grand master and open his mouth. Zhang then put two fingers down Li's throat and extracted from his mouth a fox the size of a small cat.

The fox then spoke: "Elder Sister, I came to help you, but unfortunately I've been captured. Please be careful and whatever you do don't come out."

From inside Li's stomach came a reply. "All right, I'll be careful."

It was only then they realized that two demons were living in poor Li's stomach. Grand Master Zhang took the fox fairy, sealed it in a jar, and threw it into the nearby river.

After the expurgation of the fox, Li's condition seemed to improve a little. However, it wasn't long before the voice from his stomach was heard again: "In a previous life you and I were enemies. When I had trouble finding you again, I begged help from my friend the fox fairy.

"I certainly didn't mean her to come to any harm. How can I ever forgive myself for her demise? How can I ever be in peace? I'll never forgive you for causing her death."

After this speech, Li experienced terrible pains in his stomach.

With the situation worsening again, the grand master asked the magicians for their prognosis. One of the magicians took out a magic mirror and shone it into Li's stomach, then stated: "We're not dealing with a demon. This is the ghost of someone who was wronged by Scholar Li in a previous life. I am sorry, but we have no power to cure this type of affliction."

This news was then passed to the governor by Grand Master Zhang. Since there was no other recourse, Li was sent back to his family to rest.

Sadly, it was not long before he died.

*Subduing a Fox Fairy*

## *The Immortal Fox Fairy Hangs Itself*

On Pingshi Street, Jinling, the Zhang family have a residence. On the western side of the house is a three-roomed study. The rooms are kept completely empty and firmly locked, because they are rumored to be haunted by the ghost of a woman who hanged herself there.

One day an elegant and apparently rather affluent young scholar came looking for accommodations. Mr. Zhang told him that they had no spare rooms.

The young scholar was clearly unhappy with this response and said rather aggressively, "Since I have already decided to live here, it would be far better for you if the rooms were willingly offered. I can make your life miserable, you realize."

As soon as Zhang heard this strange response he realized that he must be dealing with some sort of fox fairy. Thinking quickly, he said, "In that case, you are welcome to use the three rooms on the western side of the house."

Zhang secretly hoped he might be able to use the fox to expel the ghost. The young scholar was cheered by this news and before taking his leave he thanked Zhang with a bow.

The next day Zhang could hear laughter coming from the haunted rooms and happily noted that the fox fairy had taken up residence. He made sure there was plenty of food and wine at the fox's disposal.

After about a fortnight, the sounds of merriment suddenly ceased. Assuming that the fox fairy must have left, Zhang went to the study. He opened the door and peered into the silent rooms.

There, hanging from a roof beam, was a yellow fox.

# *Ghosts Hate Poverty*

In Yangzhou, a man by the name of Luo Liangfeng boasted that he could actually see ghosts, and insisted that every evening at dusk they wandered the streets in huge numbers. He said that ghosts particularly liked to live around wealthy families.

The ghosts were generally a few feet shorter than an average adult, and instead of having distinct facial features their heads were simply puffs of a black smoky substance. Whether walking around or leaning up against walls, these creatures kept up an incessant chatter.

The places where these ghosts preferred to gather for their evening strolls were usually crowded with people. The warmth of human activity was a form of comfort and sustenance.

Yang Ziyun explained their habits in more detail: "Ghosts especially like to reside near the houses of the wealthy and powerful. They can pass straight through walls and windows and even straight through a human body. Nothing can stop them. If they encounter someone who can actually see them, then they concentrate their energies on bewitching this intruder in a ghostly revenge.

"Poorer families are very rarely troubled by ghosts, because ghosts don't want to live in such cold and miserable surroundings. In fact, there's an apt local saying to the effect that 'I'm so poor that even ghosts wouldn't want to come and live with me.' "

# *Xiao Fu*

In the north of Yi County there lived a woman by the surname of Wang. One night, while in a deep sleep, she dreamed that a beautiful woman came to her bedside and told her she was in fact not a woman at all. Indeed, according to this ghostly visitor, Mistress Wang was really a young man and moreover one with whom the young ghost was rather keen on getting into a relationship.

"My name is Xiao Fu and when I was alive I worked as a maid for the Chen family from Panyu County," the ghost explained.

"In your previous life, you were also a servant for this Chen family. We two were lovers and had already arranged several secret rendezvous when our romance was discovered. We were forbidden to see each other ever again.

"Soon after this I died from the grief of being parted from you. Our love never came to fruition and our fate was never resolved, so I have come to you tonight to resume our unfulfilled romance."

When Mistress Wang awoke the next morning she had become quite crazed. She told her husband that she no longer wished to live with him and promptly moved to separate quarters. She became prone to laughing and talking to herself in the strangest ways. It was as if Mistress Wang had forgotten that she was a woman, because her speech was filled with the ribald obscenities of a man.

After this strange behavior had been going on for a while, the ghost Xiao Fu revealed herself during the daytime to the rest of the family. Naturally, they tried to evict this ghostly presence from their household, but nothing could persuade Xiao Fu to leave.

One day a neighbor's house caught fire and Xiao Fu alerted the Wangs, preventing certain disaster. From then on, the Wang family adopted a kinder attitude toward Xiao Fu. To show their gratitude they decided to invite her to join their household on a permanent basis.

The next year passed peacefully. Then one day, out of the blue, Xiao

Fu told Mistress Wang that she would be leaving. Xiao Fu explained that their love had been fulfilled and she was now eligible for reincarnation.

She embraced Mistress Wang for the last time and sobbed, "My love, we'll never see each other again!"

After Xiao Fu's departure, Mistress Wang's behavior returned to normal—her insanity was instantly cured.

# *A Jeweled Pagoda Formed by Ghosts*

Old Qiu was a native of the city of Hangzhou who made his living selling cloth in and around the district. One day, after squaring accounts with a client, he called at an inn, hoping to rest before making the long journey home. Unfortunately, the inn was full.

Wang mulled over his options and decided that since the road ahead was rather bleak and desolate he would have a chat with the proprietor and try to work something out.

On hearing Qiu's predicament the innkeeper said, "How tough are you? Do you have the nerve to stay in a haunted room?

"There are some rooms over by the back wall that we once used for gambling—throwing dice and the like—but nobody has stayed in them for a long time. I'm afraid they really are haunted. I personally wouldn't recommend that you stay there."

"I've traveled over twelve thousand miles during my lifetime. I don't see why I should be afraid of ghosts," Old Qiu replied.

And so, carrying a candle, the innkeeper escorted Old Qiu through to the back of the compound. Along the back wall, a couple of hundred yards from the main building, lay a line of huts. From the outside the huts appeared clean and tidy, and when Qiu went inside to complete his inspection he found to his delight that the rooms were each furnished with a table, chair, bed, and curtains.

With his customer happy, the innkeeper excused himself and returned to the main building.

It was a sultry night, so Qiu decided to sit outside to work on his accounts.

The moon cast a faint light upon the courtyard, and in the semidarkness Qiu gazed as if in a trance upon what seemed to be a human figure flitting by just a few yards away. He suspected it was a thief intent on illicit gain, but then, as he concentrated his gaze, another shadow flashed past.

Within a short time he had seen twelve such figures flitting back and forth like butterflies circling flowers. The movement was a constant, fluid dance of light and shadow.

Focusing carefully, Old Qiu discovered to his surprise that each shadowy figure was a beautiful woman.

"Men are usually frightened by the hideous appearances of ghosts, but seeing such visions of loveliness, I can only wonder at your beauty!" he said out loud.

His curiosity aroused, Qiu settled back to pay full attention to the dancing figures. Before long, two ghosts knelt at his feet and another clambered up onto his shoulders. Eventually, a total of nine ghosts climbed up one after another and formed a pyramid. To complete the formation, another of the ghosts floated up and stood at the top. The final effect was like that of the jeweled pagodas seen in theaters around town.

But then in an instant the ghosts were transformed. Each one placed a noosed rope around its neck. Their hair grew matted and their bodies gradually elongated, finally reaching over a foot in length.

When he saw this transformation Qiu laughed and said, "When you were beautiful, you were far too beautiful, and now that you're ugly, you are far too ugly. Your transformations are just as inevitable as the potential for change in life itself. Now I would like to see how you folks bring this show to a close."

At this the ghosts cackled with laughter, assumed their original forms, and quickly dispersed.

*Cards and Dice*

# *The Land Without Doors*

Lü Heng was a native of Changzhou and made his living selling imported merchandise. His work often took him on long sea voyages to foreign lands and it was on one of these trips, in the year 1775, that the boat in which he was traveling encountered a ferocious storm.

The boat sank and everyone except Lü perished. Lü survived by clinging to a piece of timber from the wreck, and in this perilous state he was swilled around the oceans and buffeted mercilessly by the waves, until eventually he was washed up on the shores of a very strange land.

As he later discovered, everyone in this land lived in buildings that were either three or five stories high. Each level was designated for a separate generation of the family. In the three-story buildings, the grandparents would occupy the third floor, the father's generation the second, and the son's generation the first. In the five-story buildings the top floor was occupied by the great-great-grandparents, and so on.

The buildings had no doors at all, just door frames, and although the people were extremely wealthy, burglary and robbery were unknown. When Lü Heng first arrived he was naturally unable to communicate with the locals. Consequently, he became adept at getting his meaning across with gestures in a rudimentary sign language. After a while he picked up a smattering of the local language and when he explained to his hosts that he was a citizen of China, they treated him with great courtesy and generosity.

It was customary in this nation to divide one day into two days. That is, the people would wake at dawn, go to work, and carry out any necessary business until noon. After this time, they would return home to sleep.

Later in the afternoon the second day would begin. Work would continue until about nine o'clock in the evening, when the people returned home to sleep again.

One of the consequences of this custom of doubling the days was that the people were twice the age they would be in China. These who said they were ten years old would be five years old in China and similarly those who said they were twenty would be only ten.

The village where Lü Heng had been washed ashore was about a thousand miles from the capital and so he didn't have a chance to visit it. There were, of course, local officials but these were very few.

Prominent among these local leaders were those officially titled Baluo, who were responsible for law and order. Lü was never able to ascertain the exact nature of the Baluos' status within the government hierarchy.

Marriages were arranged by mutual consent of the man and woman —if they liked each other, then they would marry. However, the choice of a partner was restricted by category. Everyone was placed in a certain group—beautiful, ugly, old, young—and when it came time to marry, people would select a partner from within their own group. This system reduced the likelihood of marital problems. Most significantly, tragedies resulting from unhappy romances were unknown.

Their judicial system was equally interesting. If, for example, you were responsible for breaking someone's foot, then your punishment was to have your own foot broken. If you injured someone's face, then the same would be done to you—criminal injuries and punishments matched identically, without exception. Similarly, if you raped a young girl, then her father would have the right to rape your daughter. If you had no daughters, then a wooden model of a man, complete with erect penis, would be constructed and you would be buggered by this wooden figure.

Lü lived in this strange land for a good thirteen months. Eventually a chance southerly wind blew up and he was able to catch a boat and make his way back to China. Old seafarers call this island the Land Without Doors, but it appears to have no sustained contact with China.

# *Scholar Song*

In Suzhou there was an inspector by the name of Song Zongyuan. A distant cousin of Song's who had been orphaned since early childhood was sent to live with an uncle. The uncle was extremely strict with Song's cousin and at the age of seven the boy was sent to study with the village teacher.

One day when he should have been studying the young cousin sneaked out to watch a dramatic performance in town. Someone saw him dodging class and told his uncle.

Too scared to return to his uncle's home, the boy ran off to Mudu Village and survived for a while as a beggar.

Eventually a man by the name of Li took pity on him and invited him home. From then on he worked in Mr. Li's coin shop and lived with the Li family. He was a very hardworking lad and won the affection of Mr. Li for his industry. Li decided to reward the boy and eventually gave him one of the maids, a girl by the name of Zheng, for a wife.

After nine years in Mudu Village, Song's cousin had become quite wealthy. He decided to go into the city and burn some incense as an offering of thanks to the gods.

On his way to the temple he happened to run into his uncle. Realizing he would not be able to hide the truth, he explained everything. Once the uncle found out his nephew had become quite wealthy, he immediately ordered the young man home with the intention of marrying him to someone more suitable than the maid.

At first the young man refused. "I can't leave my wife—she has just given birth to a daughter."

His uncle became furious and shouted, "We are part of a great clan! How dare you take this maid for your wife?" He forced his nephew to agree to divorce his wife.

When the Li family heard what had happened, they hoped that if they adopted the maid as their own daughter and put up a dowry as part of a formal wedding, the couple would be able to avoid divorce. The uncle refused and immediately wrote up the divorce documents and sent them to Mistress Zheng. His nephew was then forced to marry a young lady from the Jin family.

When Mistress Zheng received the divorce papers she was absolutely devastated. Carrying her baby daughter to the river, she jumped in and both were drowned.

Three years later Mistress Jin gave birth to a daughter. Not long after, the uncle went out in his sedan chair to visit a local bureaucrat. All of a sudden a tremendous wind gusted into his sedan chair, tearing aside the door curtain. When his family next saw him he was dead. It appeared he had been choked, because his neck was bruised with the telltale fingermarks of strangulation.

That night Mistress Jin had a dream that a woman with unkempt hair and blood dripping from her nostrils spoke to her: "I am the young maid Zheng. Your husband acted heartlessly when he obeyed his evil uncle's instructions to divorce me. I vowed to remain chaste after the divorce and jumped to my death in the river.

"Today I took revenge on that evil uncle, and later I will come and get your husband.

"None of this was your fault, so you have no reason to be afraid. But I cannot let your daughter live. A daughter for a daughter, that's justice."

As soon as Mistress Jin woke, she told her husband of the dream. He was terrified and quickly went out to ask his friends for advice.

One friend said: "The Daoist monk at Xuanmiao Monastery is supposed to be able to write charms that exorcise ghosts. Why don't you ask him to perform some magic on your behalf and have her locked up in Fengdu? I'm sure you'll be all right then."

So the young man sought out the monk and paid a large sum of money to ensure this ghost would be imprisoned. On a piece of yellow paper the monk wrote the woman's date of birth and all other particulars of her life history. He then invoked some magic charms and she was henceforth imprisoned in Fengdu.

There were no more strange events in the house until one day three years later. The young man was sitting at the window reading when he looked up to see Zheng approaching him and cursing. "I got my revenge on your uncle first because I knew that the injustice had been spawned by him.

"I was planning on getting you later because it wasn't your idea to divorce me, and besides, I still had some affection for you. But then you took the matter into your own hands and had me imprisoned in Fengdu. Where's your conscience?

"My period of imprisonment has just ended. I made a formal complaint to the city god and he has praised me for my virtue. What's more, he has granted permission for me to take my revenge. How do you plan to get out of this one, huh?"

The young man went instantly mad and eventually lost consciousness. All around the room, household items were being smashed for no apparent reason. Doorknobs, sticks, brooms—everything was flying through the air.

Everyone in the house was absolutely terrified. The family quickly sent for some monks, but they proved unable to expel the ghost from the house. Within ten days Song's cousin had died, and ten days after his death his daughter passed away.

His wife, however, was perfectly all right.

# *Scholar Zhuang*

Ye Xiangliu, a provincial scholar famous for his filial piety, once told me a strange tale regarding the household of a friend of his, a Mr. Chen. Chen had hired a scholar by the name of Zhuang to be the family's private tutor.

At dusk one August evening Zhuang's two charges, the young Chen brothers, were sitting in their study engaged in a game of chess, their studies being over for the day. For a while scholar Zhuang observed the game, but gradually he tired of this and decided to make his way home.

His home was about a mile from the Chen residence and separated from it by a bridge. While crossing the bridge Zhuang tripped and fell. He brushed himself off and hurried on his way.

When he finally did reach home, however, he couldn't get in. Nobody responded to his repeated knocking, so in frustration he decided to go back to the Chen residence.

The young Chen boys were still intent on their game of chess, so Zhuang strolled out into the courtyard. At the far end of the garden he noticed a small doorway, which to his great surprise led to another courtyard, this one filled with banana palms.

"Mr. Chen has such a beautiful house and yet he hardly has time to appreciate it," he sighed.

He walked up some steps towards a pavilion and there he saw a beautiful young woman giving birth. Zhuang found this vision of beauty and fecundity immensely desirable but he restrained himself, thinking, "I shouldn't be in the inner quarters of my master's house. It would be quite scandalous if I stayed to watch such a private event!"

Thus resolved, he hurried back to the boys' chess game. At one point the younger Chen brother was poised to defeat the elder, who remained oblivious to the threat, concentrating as he was on another section of the board. Zhuang tried to tell him about the danger, but much to his surprise the boy ignored his advice, although he appeared rather startled by Zhuang's intervention.

The game resumed and the boys continued to ignore Zhuang. The frustrated tutor then shouted, "You'll lose the game if you don't heed my advice!"

Pointing at various positions on the board, Zhuang tried again to explain the danger to the older boy. At this, both brothers jumped to their feet in terror. A lamp fell to the floor, and they ran as fast as they could into the house. This alarming behavior left Zhuang in a quandary, but finally he decided that the best thing he could do was head back home again.

While crossing the bridge Zhuang again tripped and fell. He resumed his walk home and knocked at the door, wondering if he would be able to rouse anyone. This time someone did wake up to let him in, but his family were greatly confused when he proceeded to abuse them for not answering his previous knocking.

Pleading innocence they said, "We didn't hear anything! There was no knocking!"

When he returned to the Chen residence the next morning he saw that the lamp in the study still lay on the floor and the chessboard remained unchanged. Poor Zhuang was thoroughly confused and it was in this bewildered state that his charges found him.

They narrated the strange events of the previous night, saying, "After you left us some very strange things happened. While we were playing chess a ghost sneaked in to scare us. It even knocked over the lamp."

Zhuang was incredulous. He explained to the senior Chen how he had tried to suggest chess moves to the boys.

"We didn't see you come back," they exclaimed.

"But I have evidence," Zhuang argued. "I saw a young woman about to give birth in the pavilion in the garden over the back wall."

"But we don't have a garden pavilion and we certainly don't have any such woman in the house!" Chen laughed.

"But it's there, behind that veranda!" Zhuang persisted.

Zhuang led Chen to the veranda, but when they reached the place where the garden should have been Zhuang found only a small earthen door leading to a modest vegetable garden.

In the western corner of the yard was a pigsty with a sow and her litter. Of the six newborn piglets, one had died.

At that moment Zhuang understood what had happened. When he tripped on the bridge the first time his soul had been knocked clean from his body. When he fell the second time his soul reattached itself.

Had he not been able to restrain his lust at the sight of the beautiful woman, he himself would certainly have become a pig.

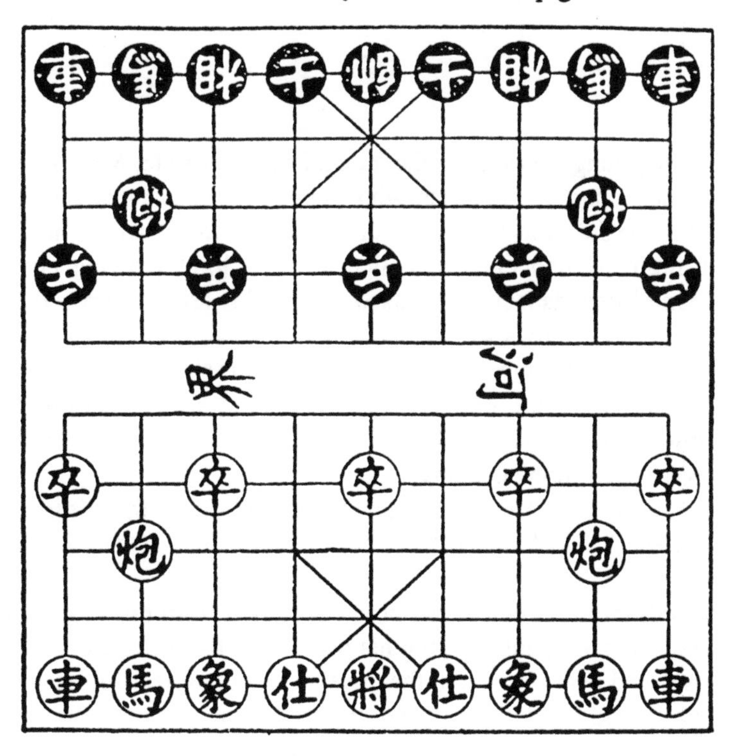


*Chess Set*

# *Little Mischief*

One of the young servants of the Yongzhou magistrate, Mr. En, was a mischievous, cheeky sort of lad who came to be nicknamed Little Mischief. His sole duty was to keep the magistrate's study clean and tidy.

One night he happened to notice a bright light glowing near the eaves. On closer inspection he discovered to his great surprise that the light was produced by a single tiny firefly.

Later that hot summer's evening while he was stretched out naked in bed, he felt something crawling and scratching around his groin. He felt around and discovered that it was the exceptionally bright firefly he'd seen earlier in the evening.

"My penis must be something marvelous! Even this little insect can't resist it!" He laughed to himself, then rolled over and went to sleep.

It wasn't too long before the boy was roused from his slumber by a soft, delicate hand gently plying his penis. The hand stroked firmly up and down and every now and then pushed gently at the tip. He tried to move but found himself paralyzed. Before he knew it, a woman's body had pressed down on him and he was having intercourse. After what seemed like quite a long time, Little Mischief ejaculated and fell into a deep sleep.

The next morning he woke exhausted. All the same, he relished his night of pleasure. Hoping the experience would be repeated, he kept it to himself.

That evening he took special pains to wash himself and then jumped eagerly into bed, once again completely naked.

Around the second watch the firefly began to glow, but this time more strongly than before. In the dim light it cast, Little Mischief could see a beautiful woman slowly approaching him. He was ecstatic and walked over to embrace her. The two lovers then fell onto the bed to relive the previous night's pleasures.

Later, Little Mischief asked her name and she replied, "My name is Miss Yao. My father used to be a magistrate here, so this magistry was my old home. Unfortunately, when I was only eighteen I fell in love. But the romance turned sour and I pined away and died. Pear blossoms were my favorite flower, so I asked my mother to bury me beneath the pear tree just outside. When I saw you, so young and virile, I couldn't resist."

Little Mischief listened to this lengthy reply with growing trepidation. When it finally dawned on him that he was sleeping with a ghost, he picked up his pillow, tossed it at the woman, and ran out shouting, screaming, and banging on doors.

Thinking there must be a fire or some other dreadful calamity, everyone ran out, only to stop in their tracks at the sight of the naked Little Mischief. The women weren't at all sure whether to continue to evacuate their rooms or to run back inside to hide their embarrassment.

Eventually the master emerged and in rather impatient tones demanded an explanation for the disturbance.

Little Mischief rattled off his tale without omission or exaggeration. He was advised to rub himself with cinnabar to ward off the ghost, and as an extra precaution he was told to put his pants back on.

The next day the magistry people dug up the ground that the foot of the pear tree. Surely enough, at its base they found a coffin. They opened it to discover the fully preserved body of a beautiful young woman. They resolved to burn the coffin and rebury the ashes.

From this day on, Little Mischief lost his mischievous, cheeky manner and became an honest, hardworking servant.

His colleagues teased him, saying, "Little Mischief has had all the mischief knocked out of him. Your type should be introduced to ghosts more often!"

# *Commander Wang*

The military commander of Shandong's Jining region was a man by the name of Wang. One night he dreamed that the famous general Zhou Chang of the Guandi temple at the southern gate said to him, "If you renovate the Guandi temple you will receive five thousand caddies filled with gold."

Wang, of course, was not at all inclined to believe in such a dream, but the next night he had a similar dream.

This time he was visited by the great general Guan Ping, who said, "Zhou Chang is one of us. More important, he is one of the most honest people you will ever meet, so you shouldn't doubt his words.

"The five thousand caddies of gold that he promised are waiting for you under the statue's incense altar. If you come tonight while it's dark, you'll be able to pick up all five thousand."

Naturally, Wang was extremely excited at this news. At the same time, he was quite scared at the thought of dealing with such powerful spirits. He ran through the situation in his mind. "If there really is gold hidden under the altar, then maybe I should go and claim it as my own."

Thus resolved, he called his son to accompany him, took some sacks in which to carry the treasures home, and set off for the temple. Arriving nearly at dawn, they saw a black fox sleeping at the foot of the altar. Its slumber disturbed the fox looked up at them with piercing eyes that glittered like gold.

Commander Wang then understood his mission. "Guandi has ordered me to expurgate this demon!"

So, with the help of his son, he bound the fox with rope, stuffed it in a sack, and proceeded home.

Along the way a voice came from within the sack: "I am an immortal fox and yesterday I got drunk and accidentally vomited all over Guandi's temple. In his anger he called you in a dream to come and get rid of me, but I regret my crime—it was only a temporary lapse.

"As you can see, I have been vigilant in cultivating myself for more than a thousand years, so won't you please let me out of this sack? I would make it worth your effort."

Wang asked in jest what benefit he could possibly gain, and the fox replied, "You will receive five thousand caddies of gold by your next birthday."

From this reply Wang realized that the promise made to him by the two great generals, Zhou Chang and Guan Ping, was to be fulfilled, so he immediately released the fox.

It leaped to the ground and instantly transformed into a white-haired old man. The man wore a scarf around his neck that fluttered out on either side, his speech was gentle, and he had a sophisticated air. All in all, the old man appeared both refined and friendly.

Back home, Wang prepared a feast in the old man's honor and the two chatted on and on about the state of the world and what it was all coming to. Near the end of the conversation Wang asked how a humble regional commander such as himself could possibly be given five thousand caddies of gold.

The fox replied, "There are numerous extremely wealthy people in Jining, and each is more evil and immoral than the next. I'll choose a few of the worst offenders and start a campaign of terror to scare them—throwing bricks around, smashing their roof tiles, and the like.

"For good measure, I'll give them all a dose of fever and headaches. They'll soon call up a few mystical Daoists and exorcists for protective charms and incantations.

"Now this is where you come in. I want you to go to their houses and tell them that you'll rid them of the demons with some of your own protective charms.

"Write a few silly characters on some paper, then burn it and toss it into the air. That will be the sign for me to move on to someone else's house. We'll repeat the process for the next month and watch as the gold caddies sent by your grateful neighbors pile up .

"Just be warned, though—once you've reached five thousand caddies you must stop, because after all you are only a regional commander. Once my debt to you has been repaid you'll not see me again."

Sure enough, several families in Jining City were terrorized by a supernatural force. It seemed as if there would be no end to the chaos.

However, just when the afflicted families were at their wits' end Commander Wang would roll up, perform his rituals, and the chaos would instantly cease.

After the month was out he had indeed accumulated five thousand caddies of gold. Two hundred of these he put towards renovating the Guandi temple, taking special care to make offerings to Generals Zhou and Guan.

He then put in a request for early retirement on the grounds that his health was failing. This was duly granted and he returned to his native village. To this day, Commander Wang lives a prosperous and peaceful life.

*Charm to Ward Away All Evil*

# *The Sea Monster of Jiangxi*

A Jiangxi man by the name of Xu Hanfu tells the story of a local fisherman who trapped fish and turtles by chanting incantations over the water.

He would walk towards the water's edge chanting his mysterious incantations, and lo and behold, the waves would rise up and dump the sea creatures onto the shore. The fisherman would then stroll along picking and choosing which of the creatures he wanted to take home that day. He was careful to take only what was needed for his own consumption.

One day, just as he was about to begin his incantations at a huge lake, a creature suddenly rose from the water. It was the size of a rhesus monkey and had eyes of gold and claws of jade, and from its mouth protruded large fangs. It moved aggressively towards the fisherman and made as if to grab him. In response he covered his head with his pants. The sea monster then jumped onto the poor fisherman's shoulders and proceeded to scratch and claw at his trousered head. Eventually the fisherman fainted and fell to the ground, blood gushing from his head.

When the other people on the shore realized what was happening, they rushed over to help. At the sight of this crowd descending upon him, the sea monster cawed like a crow, jumped ten feet into the air, and made off into the sea. The people weren't keen to chase this ferocious monster, so they gave the wounded fisherman all their attention.

When he regained consciousness he explained the sea monster's attack. "This sea monster regards all the fish and turtles of the lake as his own sons and grandsons. As I have eaten his offspring, he has come to take revenge. As you can see, it has extremely sharp claws. It uses these claws to smash the skull of its prey, and that's why I put my trousers over my head.

"If you don't cover your head it will certainly kill you. In any event, I must thank you all for your help."

# *The Sparrows Repay a Debt of Kindness*

There once lived a man by the name of Zhou Zhixiang. Zhou loathed seeing caged animals, and whenever he got the chance he would release them. He had a special affection for sparrows and would often put grain along the eaves of his roof to feed them.

When he was only middle-aged he lost his sight, but this didn't prevent him from continuing to feed the sparrows as before. Then one day, Zhou suddenly died.

His distraught family kept a constant vigil by his body because his heart and head still felt warm to the touch. After four days and four nights Zhou regained consciousness and told his anxious family the following tale.

"It was dusk and I found myself walking out of the house towards a field all on my own. There was absolutely nobody around. I remember being scared, so I quickened my pace, and after walking dozens of miles, I reached the outskirts of a city. Once again the place was completely desolate and not a light could be seen from any of the windows.

"Out of the gloom came an old man, leaning heavily on a walking stick. I recognized him as my old, dead father and I knelt down before him and cried.

"Father asked me, 'Who sent you here?'

"I replied, 'I lost my way and happened to end up here.'

"Father then gave the cryptic reply 'Oh well, so be it.'

"He led me farther into the city and we walked until we reached a government building. An old man dressed in the Daoist style, complete with head scarf, walked out to greet us, and as he came closer I realized that it was my grandfather.

"When he recognized me, he looked quite alarmed and he proceeded to reprimand father: 'How can you be so stupid! Bringing your own son to a place like this!' He promptly sent father away.

"Next thing I knew, Grandfather had taken my hand and was leading me down the street.

"Suddenly two fierce-looking prison officers appeared and shouted at us in a most terrifying manner: 'Once you've come here, you can never go back!'

"They made as if to grab me and Grandfather tried to fight them off. Then all of a sudden, millions of sparrows descended upon us from the west. They set about pecking the two prison officers, who quickly fled in terror.

"Grandfather and I continued our journey with the sparrows accompanying us all the way, forming a protective barrier. After we had walked several dozen miles Grandfather suddenly whacked me on the back with his cane and said, 'You're home now,' and the next thing I knew, I was back here. It was like waking from a dream."

Old Zhou regained his sight after this extraordinary journey and has kept in perfect health right up to this day.

# *Quan Gu*

On Dang Mountain there was a teahouse run by a beautiful young woman called Quan Gu. Her skin was fair and she was lithe and slender.

When she was nineteen she had an affair with her neighbor, an equally handsome young man by the name of Chen. Some local hooligans happened to discover their illicit affair and threatened to expose it.

Chen was from a wealthy family and he gave them a hundred gold pieces to keep the affair a secret. Somehow the officers at the magistry got wind of the deal and decided they'd take a cut.

Having the money in their hands, these hooligans weren't happy to part with any of it. A fight ensued and they were arrested and imprisoned. Chen and Quan's affair was exposed.

The head magistrate regarded himself as a proud neo-Confucian who maintained a strict moral order among the populace. He promptly ordered that Chen be given forty strokes of the cane. When Quan heard the verdict she cried and wailed, begging the magistrate to show mercy. She lay on Chen's outstretched body declaring that she would take the beating in his place.

The magistrate was scandalized by her reaction. Deeming Quan to be a shameless woman, he ordered that she also be given forty strokes.

The officers charged with administering her punishment had been slipped some money by Chen and decided to go easy on her. In any case they were reluctant to beat Quan's soft, supple, tender flesh. So while they did perform the caning, they applied very little strength in their strokes.

Unfortunately, the magistrate's anger was not slaked by the beatings and so he ordered that her hair be cut and her tiny slippers be removed from her bound feet and placed on his bench. Everyone in the courtroom who so desired was allowed to fondle the slippers, by way of warning to others. Eventually, the shoes were locked in the officer's safe. The magistrate then put Quan up for sale as a concubine and declared the case closed. His logic was that such a humiliating punishment would be a lesson to everyone in the prefecture.

Chen, still in love with Quan, bribed a local man to arrange for her purchase. Quan and the young Chen then married, but before the month was out the police and a few petty officials from the magistry were threatening to expose the subterfuge to the magistrate, so Chen had to pay another bribe.

Eventually the gossip surrounding the newlyweds reached the magistrate's ears anyway. His fury was unbounded and he ordered the immediate arrest of Quan and Chen.

This time Quan realized she would probably not get off as lightly as before, so she slipped some grass matting into her underpants to protect her buttocks from the cane. But the magistrate's keen eyes spied the bulge and he demanded, "What is that bulge on your bottom?"

He had the attendants rip off her pants and inspected both the padding and her buttocks. The Magistrate then ordered that her bare buttocks be caned under his personal supervision.

When Chen tried to stop the beating the magistrate turned on him and tattooed his face, slapping him back and forth about a hundred times. Chen's original punishment of forty strokes was then administered. He struggled home and in less than a month had died of his injuries. Quan was once again put on the market and sold as a concubine.

The day after the beatings, the magistrate was approached by a provincial-level scholar by the name of Liu. Now Liu was an upright sort of man and he found the events of the previous day intolerable. He decided to make his opinion known to the magistrate in person:

"Yesterday, when I came into town, I heard that you were going to be beating some criminals. I assumed that you would be punishing some great robbers or notorious thieves so I came over to have a look. I certainly did not expect to find a young woman with her undergarments removed being beaten.

"Such a delicate body as that, with those soft, small, curved, snow-white buttocks would not even stand the heat of the sun, let alone forty strokes of the cane. Even after the first stroke her buttocks were reduced to a pulp—like a rotten peach. All these youngsters did was to have an affair! Why did you treat them so harshly?"

The magistrate replied, "Quan Gu is a beautiful young woman. If I hadn't carried out the beating then people all around would say I was a sex maniac. The young man Chen is from a wealthy family. If I hadn't beaten him, then people would say I had been bribed."

Liu's response to this explanation was, "An official should deal with his subjects as a parent deals with a child. You have mutilated and murdered just to win a good reputation. What is it all for? In the end you will receive your just desserts."

Scholar Liu then flicked his scarf and marched out of the magistry. From that day on he cut all ties with the magistrate.

Before a decade had passed, the magistrate was transferred to Songjiang. One day, as he sat in his office having lunch, his servant saw a young man leap in through the window. Before anyone knew what was happening, the intruder slapped the magistrate's back three times and escaped.

The magistrate instantly complained of sharp pain in his back and couldn't even finish his lunch. When his manservant examined the magistrate he saw that his back had swollen out about a foot. The swelling rose in two mounds, which were divided by a small crevice—it looked exactly like a pair of human buttocks. His family immediately called for the local doctor, but the prognosis was not good. "There's not a lot I can do for him. His back already looks like the pulp of a rotten peach."

When the magistrate heard these words bile rose in his throat. Within ten days he had died.

## *A Ghost Is Chased Off by a Ghost*

In Dongcheng there lived a married couple by the names of Zuo and Zhang. They were blissfully happy and deeply in love, but one day disaster struck. The young wife, Zhang, suddenly became extremely sick and died. Zuo sorely grieved the loss of his wife and maintained a constant vigil both day and night alongside the coffin.

The Ghost Festival, July fifteenth, arrived, and while the rest of the family were in the main hall performing the usual ritual offerings to the ghosts of their ancestors, young Zuo stayed alongside his wife's coffin, reading. Suddenly he felt an eerie, chill wind blow past. Looking up, he saw a gruesome ghostly vision rushing towards him.

He could see in an instant that it was the ghost of a woman who had hanged herself, because a rope dangled to the ground from her throat. Her hair was matted and all her orifices oozed blood.

Confronted with such a sight, young Zuo panicked and banged on the coffin, screaming to his wife's corpse: "Help me, help me, my darling, please save me!"

The young wife then sat up in her coffin and said to the ghost in a rather impatient tone, "Miserable demon, how dare you attack my husband! Have you no manners at all?!"

She then raised her arm and beat the unsuspecting ghost several times. Only then did it stagger off in retreat.

Zuo's wife then turned her attention to him. "You really are crazy. I know we loved each other but this is taking it too far. I was simply not destined to live long, and your prospects don't look that good either. By taking this devotion nonsense to such an extreme you've invited harassment from that evil ghost.

"Why don't you join me here so that we can be reincarnated as a couple who are destined to live together right through old age?"

Young Zuo thought this sounded like a good idea and gave his assent. His wife then lay back in her coffin and closed the lid.

Zuo then yelled to his parents to tell them of the strange occurrence. Arriving on the scene, they saw that the nails of the coffin had snapped in half and that part of Zuo's wife's skirt was hanging out of the coffin caught between the lid and the base.

Within the year, young Zuo had also died.

## *The Folding Immortal*

In Panshiguan there is a man by the name of Chen Yiyuan who abandoned his family to cultivate his mind in Daoist magic. He purchased a small house and spent his entire time locked up in complete isolation.

He started out refusing to eat rice or rice porridge, then he refused to eat fruit and vegetables as well, and finally his only sustenance was water from Lake Shihu. His son was responsible for bringing a jar of this water to the house each month, at which time he would find an empty teapot on the steps waiting to be filled.

One day a scholar by the name of Sun Jingzhai heard tell of this hermit. Filled with admiration at such remarkable resolve, he decided to see Chen in person. So he wrote a note requesting a meeting and left it on the lid of the teapot.

He waited anxiously for the reply, and the next day when he went to check the teapot he found a note added to the end of his own saying: "You have permission to see me on February the seventh."

Sun was ecstatic and on the appointed day he made his way to the house with Chen's son. When the door opened he was greeted by a man who didn't look a day over forty, though the son who had escorted him was already an old man.

Sun began to question the Daoist: "How should one begin to practice these Daoist arts?"

"First you must sit in a serene state and try to clear your mind of thoughts. You should keep tally of the number of thoughts that come into your mind," came the reply.

So Sun sat quietly for quite some time, until eventually Chen asked, "So how many thoughts came into your head?"

"I have had seventy-two different thoughts," Sun replied.

Chen laughed and said, "It is quite normal for one's mind to be active even though the body is still and one is trying to free the mind of thoughts.

"You have had only seventy-two thoughts during this hour—that's pretty good. I think you have the potential to learn the Dao."

Sun then asked about the importance of drinking water.

He was told, "When you are born, you come from nothing and you are quite empty. Only after eating and overindulging does one's body become heavy and puffed out. This sort of life causes one's stomach to fill with worms and other dirty parasites, and eventually one's saliva assumes the consistency of mucus.

"A person who wants to know the Dao must first clear his mouth and purify his intestines. Deprived of food, all the parasites inside the stomach will starve to death and one will become empty once more.

"At the beginning of time, when heaven and earth were created and before the appearance of the five elements, the essence of life was water. Water even preceded fire.

"Although drinking water is vital to the aspiring immortal, one must ensure it is clean mountain water, because the water from the towns and cities is dirty and polluted. Drinking such water will harm your soul and not clean it. When you drink pure mountain water you should swallow slowly and make a gurgling sound in your throat. This way the sweetness of the water is extracted.

"Eventually, you should be able to survive on only one spoonful of water a day. After practicing this for about one hundred and twenty years, your body will become light and clear and then you can even dispense with the water. You'll be able to fly through the air by breathing the wind."

"Who taught you all these secrets?" Sun then asked.

"Thirty years ago I was at Mount Tai making some offerings when I came across a young man," he was told.

"He was exceptionally handsome and had a certain spiritual aura about him. He also had a remarkable ability to predict changes in the weather.

"We traveled together for several days, and during that time I noticed that every night, just before sleeping, he would take out of his bag a small brocade casket and talk to it. This seemed extremely odd and my curiosity was aroused, so I poked a hole in the partition that separated us and watched the ritual.

"The young man placed the casket on the table, tidied his clothes and cap, then knelt and bowed to the casket. Suddenly, an old man sat up inside the casket and smiled. His white hair flowed down past his shoulders and his eyes were bright and clear. The two men talked intimately for quite some time but the only words I could pick out were, 'Someone is trying to steal the secrets of the Dao.'

"Around the third watch, the young man respectfully asked the elder, 'Would you like to sleep now?'

"The old man nodded, and the young man reached up and began folding the older man as if he was folding a silk handkerchief. He then placed the man carefully back inside the casket.

"The next morning my traveling companion revealed to me that he knew I had spied on him. He then told me about his life and agreed to take me on as his disciple so I too could learn the secrets of the Dao."

Sun decided to test Chen's claims to lightness by lifting Chen's chair. Together, Chen and his chair weighed only about thirty catties.

Eventually Sun asked permission to return to his family. He said he would like to make sure his two daughters were married before he joined Chen in seclusion. He promised to return once he had dealt with these mundane matters.

I met Sun in the Zhang Ming registry at Zhenze, where he told me his plans. It was the tenth of February, 1788, during the reign of the Qianlong emperor.

## *Demons Are Terrified of Rationalism*

In Suzhou there was a wealthy octogenarian by the name of Huang who lived alone in his huge house. One day, as he was going about his business, he glanced up and saw a young woman leaning against the doorframe staring at him.

Huang calmly assumed this to be the ghost of his young daughter who had died in the house many years earlier. Deciding that no reaction was the best reaction, Huang simply pretended he did not see her.

The next night she returned, but this time in the company of a man. On the third night, while Huang was sitting reading, he noticed the couple sitting on the roof beam above his head, staring down at him. Huang continued to pretend he could not see them and turned back to his book with an unconcerned expression.

This was too much for the male ghost. He jumped down and stood directly in front of Huang. The old man then smiled and inquired, "Are you a ghost?"

He then proceeded to lecture the ghost: "Coming here to see me now is really quite foolish. I'm already over eighty years old and it won't be long before I'm living in the same world as you. I could die at any time, so why visit me now!?

"On the other hand, if you are an immortal, then why don't you sit down here next to me and tell me about yourself."

Hearing such a rational speech from Huang, the demon burst out in a tremendous howl. The sound was so intense that the windows burst open.

The wind that rushed in from the darkness outside was chilly and damp and whipped through Huang's thin clothes. Huang called out to his servants, but by the time they had hurried upstairs to see about the commotion, the ghosts had gone.

Only a few months later two of Huang's daughters-in-law and one of his grandsons died.

Among the household servants who had survived their mistress was a young maid. Huang was concerned that she would have no protection if he also passed away, and so he presented her as a concubine to a Mr. Hua Qiucha. Eventually she gave birth to three sons.

Hua now has a position as a magistrate in Zhejiang's Linhai County. In fact, it was Hua himself who told me this strange tale.

# *Spiritual Man Luo Catches the Wrong Demon*

In the second year of the Yongzheng emperor's reign, Mr. Zhang Zhongzhen passed the royal examinations with distinction and was duly assigned the position of censor in Songjiang.

He slept on a heated bed in his study but was pestered incessantly by mice scurrying to and fro between cracks in the base of the bed. Eventually the loss of sleep became intolerable, so Zhang threw some firecrackers into the holes intending to drive the mice out. But still the mice would not leave.

He then took up his gun and shot through the cracks, but the mice behaved as if nothing had happened.

Zhang then decided there must be something inside the bed that the mice wouldn't leave, so he dismantled the bed brick by brick but could find no reason for their dedication to his bed.

The study also doubled as the bedroom for his maid, and it turned out she was regularly harassed at night by someone who wore a black cloak. This person demanded sex from the maid, and if she refused, she instantly fell unconscious.

When Zhang found out about this harassment he gave the maid a jade charm he had obtained from a spiritual man, and instructed her to place it between herself and her quilt. That night the ghost in black didn't return.

However, the night after that, it did. This time, not only did it take off with the maid's underclothes, but it also desecrated the charm. Zhang was furious, so he asked a spiritual man by the name of Luo to exorcize the ghost.

Luo set up an altar and performed his various rituals for three days. The result was the capture of a raccoon-like animal. The creature was sealed in a jar and all rejoiced, wrongly assuming their troubles had ended.

That very night the ghost returned, jeering rudely at them.

"My brother was tricked by that Daoist because he didn't know when to advance and when to retreat. It's utterly despicable! But I bet that Daoist wouldn't dare tackle me!"

His behavior that night was more licentious than ever before. Zhang called Luo back again and told him of the ghost's new threats.

"My magic works only once on each demon. I can't repeat it a second time," Luo said.

This left Zhang to sort the problem out for himself. Each evening he arranged that the young lady in question sleep in the temple of the city god for protection.

Sure enough the ghost did not harass her there. Whenever she returned home, however, she would face the same old torment.

This scenario continued for about six months. And then one snowy night, while Zhang was playing chess with a friend, a strange incident occurred. The chess game had continued deep into the night and at one point Zhang happened to open the window next to him to spit out some mouthwash.

In that instant he caught sight of a black-faced animal with yellow eyes, similar in shape and size to a donkey, crouched down in hiding under the steps. Zhang spat out his mouthwash, hitting the creature's back, then leaped out through the window intending to give chase, but the creature had already disappeared.

The next morning the maid told Zhang, "Last night the monster told me you had seen him. Now that his identity is no longer a secret, he can never return here."

True enough, the monster was not seen again.

# *The Thunder God Strikes Wang San*

In Changzhou there lived a notorious criminal by the name of Wang San. When the city appointed a new prefect, a Mr. Dong Yi, his first mission was to arrest and charge Wang San.

Word of the new prefect's plan was leaked to Wang San, and he immediately went into hiding to avoid capture.

It turned out that the very day officers arrived at the Wang household to make the arrest, Wang's younger brother, Zhai, a scholar from Wujin County, was about to be married. Just as the bride crossed the threshold of her new house, Zhai was escorted out by the police, who took him in lieu of his elder brother. Zhai was summarily locked up in the local jail to await trial the next day.

That night, Wang San sneaked back home under cover of darkness. He figured that all the guests would be gone and, more important, that the police, having made an arrest, would no longer be guarding the house. He crept into the bridal chamber where the young bride lay alone and pretending to be his brother slept the night with his sister-in-law.

When Zhai was brought before the court the next morning, it was clear to the prefect that this weakling of a scholar was no criminal. Moreover, hearing that Zhai had been arrested on his wedding day, the prefect granted him a month's pardon while the search for Wang San continued.

Zhai returned home intending to make amends with his distressed wife. It was then that she realized that the man she had slept with the previous night was not her husband. Confronted with this humiliation, she hanged herself.

When news of her death reached her family, a tremendous fuss ensued. Their demands for justice were tempered when they realized that it was through no fault of Zhai's that his wife had killed herself.

"All the items of our daughter's dowry, including clothing and jewelry, must be placed in her coffin. Then we'll let the matter rest," they said.

Zhai and the Wang family, themselves sunk in the depths of despair, were in no state to object to this request.

When Wang San heard of this settlement, however, his licentious mind started to tick over. After the burial, he tracked down the grave and dug up the coffin. When he opened the lid he found the body beneath to be still in perfect condition—it was almost as if she were still alive.

He then removed her underclothes and had sex with the corpse. After the rape he filled his pockets with all the jewelry and pearls in the coffin and made off down the road.

Then, from out of the blue came a bolt of lightning and a clap of

*Thunder God*

thunder—Wang San was hit and killed in a flash. At the very instant of his death the young woman came back to life.

The next morning, Zhai received a message from the cemetery's groundsman notifying him of what had happened. He hurried over and welcomed his wife back into the family and they resumed a normal marriage.

When the prefect heard of this strange occurrence he immediately ordered that Wang San's bones be chopped into tiny pieces and burned. The ashes were to be dispersed far and wide.

# *Memories of Suiyan*

An aunt of mine, Madam Wang, was on her deathbed suffering from a terrible illness, when all of a sudden she turned toward the wall and burst into hysterical laughter.

Her daughter asked her what had happened and she said: "I have just been told that my nephew on the Yuan side will win a scholarship to further his studies. That's why I'm so happy!"

At the time of her death I was only a young student, but sure enough, a year after she had passed away I came third in the county examinations and was awarded a scholarship.

Just after the death of my father, one of his close attendants, a Miss Zhu, fell gravely ill. In the midst of her delirium she called out, "I must go now! I must go! The master is calling me to join him on the roof."

Now Miss Zhu had not been told of my father's death, since everyone, although personally grief-stricken at his parting, was concerned that news of her master's death would cause Miss Zhu's own health to decline. Nevertheless, it wasn't long before she too had died. This event supports the ancients' claim that after death the soul rises to the roof. It is, I suppose, a quite plausible explanation.

One day my gatekeeper, Zhu Ming, suddenly died. But then, just as suddenly, he opened his eyes and came back to life. Hands outstretched, he asked for some ghost money: "I'll be needing money to cover my various entertainment expenses. Could you please burn some offerings now so that I can die in peace?"

In autumn 1754, during the Qianlong emperor's reign, I was stricken with a terrible illness. In the midst of my suffering I saw, kneeling at the foot of my bed, a little boy with a white face and a tasseled hat. He held up a piece of paper on which was written, "This family is well managed but it is a little on the small side."

I suspected that this was some sort of black humor that ghosts inflict upon those with serious illnesses, so I decided to have a bit of fun at his expense as well. At lunch I had a small portion of pepper soup and this cleared my chest considerably. So I started to recite the phrase "The poor little ghost is afraid of pepper!"

At this the child smiled at me and disappeared. Later, at the height of my fever, I felt six or seven bodies lying crisscrossing along my bed. If I lay still for too long they would shake the bed, and if I were quiet for too long they would try to get me to moan and groan.

As my fever receded the number of people lying across my bed was reduced, so that once the fever had completely passed I was alone in my bed again. From this incident on, I have always believed in the theory of the "three spirits and the six souls."

But on the other hand there are some dreams that simply can't be accounted for.

My grandfather, Yuan Danfu, loved dabbling in Daoist magic. One night he dreamed he was on a mountaintop, and there before him a banquet was taking place. It was just like the eight immortals' banquet he had seen in various paintings.

When my grandfather approached, none of these immortals would rise to greet him, so he said in jest: "There may be eight immortals but you've only fifteen legs between you."

The crippled immortal, Li, was furious at this and he took up his crutch and struck out at Grandfather. The other immortals pushed Grandfather onto his knees shouting, "Hurry up! Beg forgiveness!" But by this time the crutch had already struck my grandfather's stomach.

Cripple Li then said, "I will give you three more years, but that's all!"

Grandfather woke with a terrible fright. It wasn't long after this that he developed an egg-sized swelling on his waist, which none of the doctors seemed to be able to do anything about. Gradually the lump became putrid. Three years later my grandfather died.

That's why I am always joking, "That lousy cripple has made enemies of my entire family for all eternity, so I'll curse his portrait whenever I see it." I've not suffered any retribution yet.

My brother-in-law Wang Gongnan once dreamed that while visiting the grave of Shaobao to ask instructions from the divine beings there he was chased by an ugly, ferocious monk armed with a stick.

In a panic Gongnan fled, eventually coming across a group of several dozen monks seated in a grassy clearing. Gongnan begged for their assistance and the monks hid him in the grass, linked hands, and formed a circle facing outwards with Gongnan in the center.

His pursuer arrived and when he couldn't get through to Gongnan he said to the monks, "Why do you want to protect this heartless bastard? Move aside and let him have a taste of my stick!"

At that point Gongnan woke from his dream in terror. But nothing seems to have happened to him yet.

I remember as a young boy dreaming that I was floating down a river on a raft made of thousands of writing brushes. To date, nothing seems to have come from this dream either.

One day in early spring I had a dream that the god of war, Guandi, complete with his long, flowing beard and green gown, was hanging in midair before me. He grabbed me with his left hand and hurled a bolt of lightning at my back with his right. The lightning scorched one side

*Cripple Li*

of my body; it was agonizingly painful. When I woke from the dream, my stomach was still quite hot.

One explanation given for this dream was that Guandi was born in the year of the horse and I had passed the county examinations in another horse year. I suppose it is possible, but I'm not very convinced.

I sat the county examinations in 1732, during the Yongzheng emperor's reign. At the fifth watch of the day before the examinations were due to start, I dreamed that our old doorman, Li Nianxian, stopped me in the middle of the road. Waving his hands frantically, he implored me not to attend.

"Don't go! Don't go! If you sit the examinations this year you will fail. They are only passing a very few talented scholars this year. Wait until they plan to pass a lot of scholars before you sit the examinations."

At the time they had been passing a very wide range of scholars and so I thought that this premonition was nonsense. As it turned out I did in fact fail. Being awarded a scholarship is only the first step on the long road of the examinations.

Even at this early stage, it was clear to me that supernatural forces were at work. All the same, I did succeed in becoming a provincial candidate, went on to become a Hanlin Academician, and was promoted to the position of magistrate without any further supernatural predictions. I often wonder why.

# *The Cool Old Man*

At Mount Wutai in Shanxi Province there lived a Buddhist monk who was known by the title of Cool Old Man. During his life he took it upon himself to spread Buddhist teachings, particularly the Zen school. He was quite famous and even Premier E had studied under him. In 1726, during the Yongzheng emperor's reign, the monk passed away.

At the exact moment of his death, a child was born in Tibet. The child didn't say a word until he was eight years old. Just as his head was being shaved the boy suddenly shouted, "I am the Cool Old Man. Go quickly and tell Premier E that I am here!"

The premier summoned the boy and questioned him to verify his identity. Everything the boy said was just as the Cool Old Man would have said. The boy recognized all the premier's attendants and, addressing them by name, chatted with them as if he had never been away.

Premier E then decided to give him one last test. He presented the boy with a set of rosary beads. The boy took the beads, bowed lowly, and said, "I can't accept these beads. They are the very beads that I presented to you in my previous incarnation."

The startled premier immediately ordered that the boy be taken to Mount Wutai to resume his position as abbot.

On the way to the monastery, the party passed through Hejian Village. While there the boy sent word of his arrival to a Mr. Yuan, a Hejian local, who had been a great friend of the Cool Old Man during his previous life. When Yuan received the letter he saddled the black horse that the monk had given him, and galloped off to welcome his friend back to the region. Needless to say, Yuan was all the while in a state of considerable surprise.

When the boy saw his friend on the black horse he immediately stepped out of the carriage and embraced him, saying, "We've been apart for eight years now. Do you still remember me?" Then he stroked the horse's mane and asked, "And you, my friend, how have you been?"

The horse neighed repeatedly by way of recognition.

Eventually word of the Cool Old Man's arrival spread and soon thousands of people were lining the streets to worship this reincarnation of the Buddha.

The boy matured into a slender young man whose skin was as smooth and soft as any woman's. One day as he passed through Liulichang he caught sight of some erotic pictures hanging in an art dealer's window. The pictures showed men and women having sexual intercourse in a variety of positions. The young abbot was enraptured by this sight and promptly purchased the entire set. He proceeded on his way with his eyes glued to the pictures.

Making his way back to the monastery he passed through Baixiang, where he chanced upon a group of prostitutes. He then indulged himself, putting into practice his new-found skills.

Reaching Mount Wutai, he summoned to the monastery all the local prostitutes and courtesans as well as any good-looking young man from the district who was endowed with a huge member. From then on, day and night without stop, he sat and watched the group perform innumerable licentious acts. It was as if his desire would never be satiated, for he went so far as to use the money donated to the temple by worshipers to hire dancers and performers from Suzhou.

Eventually his behavior caused such a scandal that somebody organized a petition of complaint and sent it as a memorial to the emperor. Before the memorial had reached its destination the young abbot knew of its contents.

"Some people mistakenly believe that the world would be just as beautiful as it is now if the landscape were stripped of trees," he sighed.

The abbot sat down, fell into a deep meditative trance, and died. He was only twenty-four.

An acquaintance of mine, Li Zhuxi, was a friend of the Cool Old Man's previous incarnation. Li said that one day he had paid the old man a visit and found him dressed from the waist up as a woman, but from the waist down he was quite naked except for a flimsy cloth that covered his belly.

A man was instructed to have sex with him from behind while he had sex with a woman from the front. All around this trio people were engaged in similarly licentious acts.

Li cursed the old man, saying, "A living Buddha would never behave in such a way!"

The old man was unconcerned. "The unrestricted and unhindered acts of love between a man and a woman give rise to the essence of life itself. Indeed this is how the world came to exist. It is only those of ignorance and commonplace perceptions who are frightened and shocked by such things."

# *A Tiger Steals the God of Literature's Head*

It was June and the height of the summer heat in Shanxi Province's Xing'an City. A wedding was in process and the bride, dressed in full wedding regalia, including a heavy red veil, suffered greatly as the sedan chair made its long journey to her bridegroom's house. Indeed, so great was the heat inside the chair that by the time the wedding party reached its destination the bride had died from heat exhaustion.

The bride's distraught parents paid for a coffin even though they were unable to take the body back home with them. As a married woman their daughter was, strictly speaking, a member of her husband's family. Her coffin was placed at the rear of an old temple just beyond the city walls.

Now this coffin was not particularly sturdy and it wasn't long before rainwater from the summer downpours had seeped through the walls. The water had a cooling and nourishing effect and it soon revived the body inside.

As the bride regained consciousness she began to moan and mumble, and these noises were detected by the monk and his disciple who were responsible for maintaining the temple. They quickly lifted the coffin lid and there before them lay a beautiful woman.

They helped her out of the coffin and gave her some nourishing broth and medicinal tonic. When she was sufficiently recovered, the monks helped her back to the temple.

The disciple became fixated with the idea of making this woman his own, so he contrived to rid himself of his master. He bought some wine and got his unsuspecting master completely drunk. Once the monk was in this helpless state the disciple took up an axe and killed him. He then dragged the monk's body to the back of the temple and placed it in the bride's coffin.

Picking up the woman, the disciple carried her to a neighboring village, where he took up residence in a deserted temple built in honor of the god of literature. The disciple then grew his hair and assumed the life of a married Daoist priest.

One day after this, a tiger sprang into the temple, snapped off the head of the statue of the literature god, and carried it off into the distance. In its place the tiger left three tiny cubs. This strange event caused a huge commotion in the village, and people came from near and far to see the cubs.

Quite by chance, among the crowds that filled the temple were the woman's parents, and when they saw their daughter standing before

*God of Literature*

them their first thoughts were that she must be a ghost. When they discovered that she was quite alive, there was a tearful reunion.

Deciding that it was pointless to hide the truth, the woman told her parents of what had taken place, including the murder of the monk and her own abduction. The parents immediately filed an official complaint with the local magistrate, and after the investigation, complete with the exhumation of the monk's corpse, had confirmed their allegations, the disciple was punished according to due process of law. The woman was placed back in the care of her father and permitted to return home.

I was told this tale by a reader at the Hanlin Academy, Yan Dong-you, who had just returned from travels in Shanxi.

# *Revenge on the Warrior of the Flowers*

A man named Yang who lives in the capital is renowned for his skill in the "battle of the flower pickers." This "battle" is actually a magical sexual art whereby Yang takes a lead rod, puts it deep into a woman's vagina, then moves it in and out in time with his breathing.

He calls this technique "testing the sword." He can also control the width of the rod with his breath, making it thicker so that it rubs noisily against the walls of the vagina. Moreover, he can maintain these breathing techniques while drinking half a quart of liquor.

This sadistic form of sex generated considerable horror among the prostitutes around town.

One day Yang came to the conclusion that these special skills, impressive as they were, would not grant him eternal life. So he set about the arduous task of searching for a teacher who could impart knowledge of immortality pills.

Yang had heard that each year on the nineteenth of January, the famous Daoist monastery of Baiyun, situated outside Fucheng's city gates, was visited by an immortal. This particular monastery had been built in the Yuan dynasty in honor of Qiuzhen, a priest of amazing spirituality. People came from miles around to make offerings and burn incense, and the monastery was especially crowded on the appointed day in January.

Yang figured that this would be a likely place to start his quest, so he made the journey to the monastery to see the immortal.

When he arrived he saw a beautiful nun in the crowd of people lined up to offer incense. Yang's sharp eyes noticed that her clothes didn't move with the breeze, as did those of the others around her, so he concluded that she must be an immortal. Yang walked over and knelt at her feet, respectfully asking for her assistance.

"Are you the Mr. Yang who has mastered Daoist sexual techniques?" the nun queried.

"Yes, I am that man," Yang replied.

Hearing this she declared, "I only teach my Dao to an extremely select group. I am not interested in passing on my knowledge to ordinary people."

Even more intrigued, Yang continued to worship respectfully at her feet, begging her to take him as a disciple.

Finally the nun agreed. She led him to a secluded part of the monastery grounds and gave him two pills, saying, "We'll meet on the full moon next month. I'll give you these two pills. The first you can take now, but the second you should take just before our next meeting. Then I will teach you the secret of my Dao." After specifying the time and location of the meeting she left.

Yang dutifully swallowed the pill and instantly felt as if his whole body was burning. What's more, his desire for sex increased to an almost unbearable level. He visited brothel after brothel, and gradually gossip of his excessive sexual appetite got around until all the prostitutes in town avoided him.

When the appointed time arrived, Yang took the second pill and made his way to meet the nun.

She was waiting quietly for him and as soon as he was inside, she removed her clothing saying cryptically, "There is no secrecy between bandits. Even if you had wings you still couldn't fly. Have you heard these ancient sayings? If you want my knowledge you must first have sex with me."

Yang was greatly excited at this opportunity, and rather proud of his prowess in the "battle of the flower pickers," so he quickly joined her in bed. However, it wasn't very long before he had spent all his sperm, and he fell to the floor, limp and exhausted.

The nun got up and shouted viciously at him, "Pass on the Dao! Pass on the Dao! Evil invites an evil revenge!" She laughed a raucous laugh and left.

Yang regained consciousness at the fifth watch. Looking around, he realized he was lying in a ramshackle shed. He could make out the calls of a bean curd vendor nearby, and in his pitiful state he crawled outside. While waiting for his family to come and carry him home Yang told his tale to the bean curd vendor.

Three days later Yang was dead.

# *The Wooden Guardsmen*

In the capital, the Currency Board's main compound has a small temple dedicated to a local god. The temple is protected by the wooden statues of four guardsmen. The coppersmiths working at the Currency Board would regularly worship at the temple, since they all lived in the compound.

One night it happened that the younger men among the team had an identical nightmare. They dreamed that they were sodomized but despite the nausea and pain were unable to shout or move. It was as if their feet and hands had been bound. When they woke the next morning and rubbed their sore anuses, each discovered his own to be caked with a black mud.

This pattern continued for over a month and the coppersmiths were at a loss to know who or what was taking advantage of them.

Eventually, one of the victims, while making an offering at the temple, recognized the face of one of the wooden guards as that of the rapist. He promptly informed the others and they reported it to the magistrate. The feet of this wooden statue were then nailed down as a punishment and precaution. After this, the strange nightly visits ceased.

# *A Woman Transforms into a Man*

The Xue family from Leiyang County had a daughter by the name of Xue Mei. They betrothed her to a boy from the Huang family, but just before the wedding Xue Mei was struck by a mysterious sickness that made her dangerously ill.

While delirious she was approached by a white-haired old man. He began to massage her all over, gradually working his way down to her hips and genitals. She became very embarrassed and tried to stop him, but he continued to massage the area.

Before he left, he forcefully inserted something into her genital area. Xue Mei cried out and her worried parents came running in to see what was wrong. Then they saw that although her illness had passed she had been transformed into a man in the process.

The acting magistrate was Zhang Xizu, and he and another official, Tao Huixuan, who happened to be in the prefecture on other business, came to the Xue house to examine the girl. They officially confirmed that Xue Mei had become a man. Her voice and facial features were still those of a woman, but in her groin she had a penis and all that remained of her vagina was a crack in the skin.

The Xue family changed her name from Xue Mei to Xue Lai and so the number of sons in the household increased from two to three.

# *The Prince of Guazhou*

In Hangzhou there is a place called Da Fangbo where the Hu family lived, the two sisters-in-law sharing the same floor.

One day during the grave-sweeping festival of Qing Ming, one of the sisters-in-law noticed a small bridgelike structure on the roof. It was made from willow twigs so she assumed that the children had put it there. She used a long bamboo pole to scrape it off the roof and into the rubbish bin.

That night she dreamed that a young man dressed in the manner of a Daoist appeared before her.

"I am the Prince of Guazhou and it is my fate that I live with you and your sister-in-law," he said.

"I made a lover's bridge and placed it on your roof so that we could meet during Qing Ming. Why did you throw it away?"

From this day on, the so-called prince stayed in the women's room, taking advantage of them as he pleased.

The scandalized Hu family then called a Daoist priest to scare away the intruding demon by chanting the Jade Emperor Sutra. However, when the priest arrived the monster threw a chamber pot at him, soaking him and his sacred books in urine. The priest ran off, humiliated.

Mr. Hu then decided to hire five old women to chaperone the two younger women. Mysteriously, the old women's hair became plaited together so that they were unable to move backwards or forwards without pulling the others' hair.

This continued for over a month, until it was time for one of the women to be married to her betrothed. Mr. Hu chose an appropriate day and married her off.

The monster then confronted Mr. Hu in person, saying, "I am not fated to be with the man you have married her to, so I can't go. I could stay on here and enjoy myself with the remaining sister-in-law, but it is rather boring to have only one beautiful woman to play around with, so I think I'll just say goodbye.

"I've really caused you a lot of trouble and I have no way of repaying your generosity. But I do have an extremely beautiful young sister whom I could give to you as a concubine, if you like," he continued.

Mr. Hu asked to see the sister in question and sure enough when they went out into the hall, there stood a young girl of exceptional beauty.

Hu asked hastily how long it would take to arrange the wedding and the monster replied, "Although I am quite happy to have you as my brother-in-law, my sister doesn't want to marry you because you are old and ugly. However, if you shaved your beard she would consider marrying you."

Mr. Hu was indeed a corpulent, full-bearded man of more than fifty. He believed the monster and dutifully shaved off his beard, but after he had done so the monster merely laughed coarsely at him, leaped into the air, and flew off.

Of course, the beautiful sister never did come back.

# *Yang Er*

Yang Er of Hangzhou was skilled in the martial arts and particularly adept with his fists and his staff. One summer night while he was sitting in the cool of a rocky outcrop on a small seat carved out of the stone, he saw a tiny head emerging from a crack in a nearby rock. The hair appeared first and the face quietly followed.

The terrified Yang Er grabbed his staff and struck the protruding head, which quickly popped back into its little crevice.

While Yang Er was in his room the next day, he heard the click-clack of clogs from the floor below. He was pretty sure that this was no thief, since thieves would not be so foolish as to wear clogs. It wasn't long before the click-clack noise came up the staircase towards Yang Er's room.

At the doorway there appeared a man dressed from head to toe in white. He wore a tall hat and in his hand he held a box lantern. When the man in white saw Yang Er, he burst into a raucous cackle.

Confronted with this creature, Yang Er promptly struck him with an iron ruler, causing him to topple backwards down the staircase.

The man in white shouted angrily back up the stairs, "You call that a good thrashing! Well, wait till I get my gang onto you. Then I'll show you a thing or two!"

Yang Er called his disciples together and told them of the threats made against him by the ghost.

These rascally disciples roared with indignation and bravado. "So what if they've formed a gang? So have we! We'll defend out master! We'll go up there and beat the living daylights out of them!" they cried.

The men first had themselves a feast, eating and drinking until they were satisfied. Finally they grabbed their weapons and headed upstairs to Yang Er's room. The ghosts, however, were nowhere to be seen.

By the time the cock crowed to herald the new day, these scoundrels had all tired of their mission and fallen asleep. When they finally awoke it was too late. They found Yang Er dead on the bamboo matting in the room below.

## *Helping a Ghost Get Revenge*

The express postman in the Bureau of Salt Transport was a man by the name of Ma Jixian. In the course of his employment he had become quite wealthy, so he purchased for his son, Huanzhang, a position as a minor official.

Now the son himself became a very talented bureaucrat, and he soon grew even wealthier than his father. It wasn't long before the Ma family were millionaires.

Years passed and Jixian, now an old man, bought a concubine whose surname was also Ma. The two of them developed a deep and trusting bond. Jixian was so appreciative of his concubine's efforts that he said to her one day, in reference to his accumulated wealth of several thousand caddies of gold, "You have been such a loyal and attentive assistant in my old age that I have decided to leave you all my property when I die. I don't mind whether you stay on with my family or remarry after my death. It is up to you."

Five or six years later Ma Jixian became gravely ill and called his son to his side. "This woman has been a devoted concubine. I want all my savings passed to her when I die."

However, after his father's death Huanzhang did nothing of the sort.

He and his uncle, Mr. Wu, a former prefect in Quanzhou, plotted to ensure that the money stayed with them.

Huanzhang explained his problem to Wu, concluding, "Who would have thought that my father would want to leave all his wealth to this woman? What a dreadful waste!"

"This shouldn't be too difficult to sort out. I'll come and help you chase her out of the house," Wu responded.

Several days later Huanzhang told the concubine to leave the house where she and Jixian had lived, using the excuse that she should sit with the coffin and wait until the soul had left the body. As soon as she was out of the house, Huanzhang and his wife transferred all the dead man's possessions, including all his treasures, into their own room. They then locked the door of the old man's house.

Naturally, the concubine remained oblivious to the theft.

When the seven days of mourning were over and Ma Jixian's soul had left his body, the concubine returned to the house planning to go back to her rooms in the inner chambers and begin her life as a widow.

Mr. Wu then suddenly shouted harshly at her, "Aunty Concubine! Don't go back in there! You're too young to remain a chaste widow all your life. Why don't you pack up your things and go home to your mother? She'll find you another man! I'll make sure the young master gives you some money."

Wu then asked Huanzhang to take fifty caddies of silver to the concubine.

Huanzhang hurried out saying, "Look, I've got it all ready for you!"

But the concubine insisted that she wanted to return to her rooms.

"I'm sorry," Huanzhang said, "but this is what our uncle, Prefect Wu, has instructed. I'm sure he's not mistaken in this regard. We've packed all your belongings into boxes, so there is no need for you to go back into the house."

The concubine, accustomed to obeying the orders of her husband and stepson, was also afraid of the power of Prefect Wu. She had no option but to order a carriage and leave, barely able to suppress her tears.

Huanzhang, needless to say, was extremely grateful to Wu for devising such a scheme.

Several months later, during the preparations for the Ghost Festival of July fifteenth, the concubine decided to return to the Ma residence to make some offerings in honor of her dead husband's spirit. By this time, the money she had taken home had been squandered by her brothers and parents. On the twelfth of July, she took some incense and other paraphernalia for worship and set off for the Ma residence.

Huanzhang's wife saw her approaching and hurried out shouting abusively, "You're a shameless hussy! Coming back after you've left the family!"

Her entry to the main rooms thus blocked, the concubine was ordered to remain in the corridors that ran through the outer sections of the residence and instructed to spend the night there before making her offerings.

"You must leave as soon as you complete the worship. I won't allow you to stay a minute longer," she was told.

The concubine cried and sobbed all night long, the noise ceasing only around the fifth watch. The next day, her body was discovered hanging from a roof beam. Huanzhang bought a coffin for the body and performed the appropriate funeral rituals for her.

The concubine's family made no complaints, nor did they call for any investigation of the death, since they too were frightened of Wu's authority. For his part, Huanzhang felt uncomfortable remaining in a house where a ghost might be living, so he sold it to a Mr. Zhang and bought an even more luxurious mansion.

Mr. Zhang had been a devout Buddhist from a very young age. During his nightly prayers he often encountered the spirit of the sobbing concubine. He eventually found out what had happened. In addition to being angry at having been sold a haunted house, he was quite indignant at the injustice of the concubine's treatment.

He said to the ghost, "Mistress Ma, my family and I paid a lot of money for this house. It wasn't as if we took it by force or anything like that. The hatred you have for Mr. Wu and Huanzhang, moreover, has nothing to do with my family. How would it be if I delivered you to Huanzhang's new house myself, tomorrow night, around the second watch?"

The ghost smiled her assent and disappeared.

The next night, Zhang made a tablet for the ghost, burned incense in preparation, then delivered her to the gate of Huanzhang's new residence.

"Wait here. I'll go knock on the door," he whispered to the tablet.

He then walked over, knocked on the door, and addressed the doorman. "Has your master returned for the night?"

"Not yet, sir," came the reply.

Zhang turned to the ghost and said, "You might as well go in now and prepare to take your revenge."

The doorman laughed, thinking Zhang some sort of lunatic talking nonsense to himself, and thought nothing more of it. For his part, Zhang returned home and spent an anxious night without sleep. Even before the sun had risen the next morning he had rushed back to the Ma residence to find out what had happened.

The same doorman was standing at the entrance. Zhang asked him, "Why are you working so early?"

"You know, as soon as the master returned last night he became gravely ill. His situation is quite critical now," replied the doorman.

Zhang was terrified at this news and hurried back home. Late that afternoon he made his way back to the Ma's mansion and discovered that Huanzhang had already died. Several days later Mr. Wu also passed away.

Huanzhang had died without sons, so his property was claimed by relatives. Wu also had no descendants, so the fortunes of this line of his family also went into an immediate decline.

# *A Donkey Helps Solve a Strange Case*

This strange tale occurred in 1788 during the reign of the Qianlong emperor.

In Baoding Prefecture, Qingwan County, the Li and Zhang families were joined by the marriage of the Zhangs' son to one of the Li family's daughters.

The distance between the Li family home and the Zhangs' village was more than a hundred miles, and so the customary visit of the bride to her parents after a month of marriage was not a simple matter.

However, the new Madam Zhang made the journey, and when it came time to return she was picked up by her husband. He brought a donkey for her to ride while he walked behind.

About twenty miles from the Zhangs' village they passed through a village where the husband had a number of good friends. They got caught up in conversation and eventually Zhang suggested to his wife that she start off for home before him. The donkey knew the road so there was supposedly little danger that she would get lost.

She had gone only six or seven miles when she came to an intersection. The western path led to the Zhangs' village and the eastern path to Renqiu County.

Just as the donkey was about to cross to the western path, a carriage owned by a wealthy young Renqiu man by the name of Liu came hurtling past. It pushed the donkey off the road leaving the poor animal quite disoriented. The donkey then resumed its steady pace, but this time on the eastern path towards Renqiu, away from the Zhangs' village.

Towards dusk, the young bride began to suspect something had gone terribly wrong. Coming across the wealthy young Renqiu man, whose carriage had stopped, she nervously asked how far she was from Zhang Village.

"You're going the wrong way for Zhang Village. You should have gone west," the young man replied.

"This road goes to Renqiu. You're only a couple of dozen miles away! It's too late to stay on the road, though.

"Come with me and I'll find you lodgings for the night. In the morning I'll send someone over to see you home. How does that sound?"

There was little that Madam Zhang could do, so she muttered her tentative assent to the stranger's plan. He led her to one of his nearby properties. The tenant of the estate was a Mr. Kong and he agreed to provide a bed for Madam Zhang.

By coincidence, Kong's newly married daughter was also back visiting her parents for the first time since her marriage. Faced with a shortage of suitable beds, Kong asked his daughter if she could go back to her husband's, for the night.

"Our landlord's here and we can't offend him, so why don't you head back to your husband's, and when Liu has gone I'll come and fetch you back again."

The daughter saw the predicament her father was in, so she returned to her new husband's house. The room where she had planned to stay was then prepared for Madam Zhang and Landlord Liu. Liu's carriage driver slept outside and Madam Zhang's donkey was tied under the eaves at the eastern end of the house.

The next day at noon, when the two guests had still not emerged from behind their locked door, Kong peeked through a crack in the window to see what was going on. There lying on the bed were two headless corpses; the heads lay on the floor. The young woman's donkey had also disappeared during the night.

Kong and Liu's driver were terrified. Both men trembled helplessly in the face of this disaster.

After some time, when they had calmed down, Kong said secretively to the driver, "You're from Henan, aren't you? Why don't you grab your gear and head back home straightaway? Once the police hear about this I think we'll be lucky to get away with our lives. If you escape now to faraway Henan, you should be all right."

The driver agreed. Later that night before he packed up the carriage, he and Kong buried the bodies.

Now when her son failed to appear as expected, Liu's anxious mother promptly went to Renqiu and filed a lawsuit against the carriage driver.

Similarly, when Zhang discovered that his wife had not reached home, he suspected foul play and filed an official complaint in Qingwan against his wife's parents.

The magistrate suspected the deceased had been murdered by bandits, so instead of rushing out to arrest the accused persons he decided to do a little investigating in secret.

It turned out that a local hoodlum by the name of Guo San had been seen in the markets trying to sell a donkey that fitted the description of the missing Zhang donkey. The magistrate quickly pulled Guo in for questioning and it turned out that he and Kong's daughter had been lovers. When Guo heard that his lover was to spend a few days back at her parents' house he decided to try to see her.

When he sneaked into her bedroom he saw a man and a woman together on the bed. This sight made him wildly jealous and in a fit of rage he murdered the two while they slept before fleeing on the donkey.

The magistrate then asked Kong about the corpses and was dutifully shown the gravesites. Exhumation began, but strangely enough, only three feet below the surface there appeared the body of a bald monk. Only after further digging were the two bodies in question found.

So, with one investigation both the Liu and Zhang families' cases were solved. However, a new mystery, that of the dead monk, had emerged.

Just as the investigating party was pondering this new case the sky suddenly clouded over and it began to rain. They all hurried for shelter to an old, deserted temple not far from the gravesite.

Conversation with a few of the villagers revealed that the temple had been maintained by two monks, one the master and the other a disciple. But recently the locals had heard that the master had decided to go traveling. Strangely enough, the disciple had also disappeared around this time. On examining the corpse the villagers confirmed that this was the body of the senior monk, who was supposed to be traveling.

An arrest warrant was immediately issued for the disciple, and when they located him in Henan's Guide region he had grown his hair back and taken a wife. The two of them were running a bean curd shop.

On interrogation it emerged that the wife had been the long-time lover of the senior monk. As the disciple grew to be a man she had also taken him as her lover. Eventually she found the older man to be quite unsatisfactory, so she and the disciple jointly resolved to kill him. This achieved, they abandoned the temple and ran off to be officially married.

These two were dealt with according to the law.

# *Scholar Zhang*

There was a scholar from Hangzhou by the name of Zhang who worked as a tutor in the governor's residence in the capital. His study was situated in the garden a hundred-odd yards from the main residential buildings, and being a cowardly sort of fellow, Zhang always insisted that the houseboy responsible for tidying the study stay overnight with him.

Every night, as soon as it became dark enough to require a candle, Zhang would go straight to bed and sleep. This routine had continued unchanged for over a year until the night of the Midautumn Festival, when the moon was particularly big and bright.

The houseboy had gone out drinking to celebrate, so the garden gate was not yet locked, and Zhang, planning to admire the fullness of the moon himself, walked out into the garden. While he was strolling among the landscaped mounds and rocks he suddenly caught sight of a woman, completely bereft of clothing, walking towards him.

Her hair was tangled and her white skin was smeared with mud and grime. Zhang was absolutely terrified. He instantly assumed that he was looking at a corpse that had just dug its way out from the ground. Her eyes had an unnatural brightness and in the light of the full moon they took on a particularly frightening gleam.

Zhang ran as fast as he could back to his study, blocked the door with a wooden doorstop, and jumped into bed. Peeking fearfully out from under the covers, he could hear a tremendous banging as the woman tried to open the door.

Eventually the doorstop gave way and in walked the woman. She sat down at Zhang's desk and proceeded to tear all his books and papers to shreds. The ripping and tearing made a terrible sound and poor Zhang nearly passed out in terror.

Having destroyed his papers, she then took up his ruler and banged it repeatedly on the desk, sighing long and loudly all the while.

Zhang then really did slip into a semiconscious state and his soul was just about to quit his terrified body when he became aware that the woman was now manipulating his genitals.

"What a typical, barbaric southerner! This thing is absolutely useless! Absolutely useless!" she cursed loudly.

She then walked out and left him alone.

The next day Zhang lay in his bed stiff as a corpse in this semiconscious state. When his students tried to rouse him for lessons they received no response, so they ran back to inform the governor. Some ginger juice was poured straight down Zhang's throat and he gradually regained consciousness.

He then recounted the terrifying events of the previous night.

But the governor just laughed, saying, "That was no ghost you saw, my dear fellow. It was a servant of ours! She went crazy after losing her partner and we've had her locked up over two years now. Last night, however, she managed to escape and obviously made quite a nuisance of herself terrifying you!"

Zhang remained skeptical of this explanation, so the governor personally took him to the woman's room to see for himself. Sure enough, the woman in the room and the woman he had seen the previous night were one and the same. In an instant he felt much better, although the embarrassment of having been described as absolutely useless left him feeling rather ashamed.

The houseboy laughed at him, saying, "Lucky she thought you were useless! If she had thought it worth the effort you might have found yourself in a worse state this morning. She's prone to biting and pinching penises. Other people have had their penises nearly snapped in two after an evening in her clutches! Once she likes a fellow's organ, she keeps going at it nonstop."

# *The Reincarnation of Cai Jing*

During the reign of the Chongzhen emperor at the end of the Ming dynasty, there lived a gentleman who claimed to be the reincarnation of Cai Jing. He said that he was an officer from heaven who had fallen into the deepest of all the levels of hell. He had flashes of extreme clarity whenever anybody recited the Benevolent King Sutra.

He claimed that one of his punishments had been rebirth as a Yangzhou widow. She was forced to live on her own, maintaining a strict code of chastity, for forty years. Consequently, this gentleman had a liking for the strangest sexual activities.

He was, for instance, particularly fond of admiring the buttocks of beautiful women and the penises of handsome men. He maintained that male beauty was better admired from the front, whereas female beauty was better from a rear view. Anyone who thought otherwise he deemed ignorant of good sexual practice.

He would often dress women in men's gowns and singlets and, conversely, dress men in women's skirts and jewelry, taking great delight in groping and fondling the profusion of buttocks and penises.

His several dozen concubines and houseboys were often involved in his strange escapades as well. One game which was particularly good fun involved having everyone remove the clothing from their lower body while completely covering their heads. The trick then was to run around and guess who was who by feeling the exposed bodies.

One of the cabinet's scribes, a man by the name of Shi Jun, was very slim and good-looking, but more importantly, his private parts were quite exquisite. Our gentleman loved to suck on Shi Jun's penis and found endless delight in playing with it. Indeed, whenever this gentleman was asked for an example of his calligraphy, he would insist that Shi Jun grind the ink for him before he proceeded.

Mr. Shi's buttocks were given the nickname "handfuls of jade white brocade" and his penis was called the "immortal rosy rod" by the adoring gentleman.

*Wheel of Reincarnation*

# *Hanging onto the Ears of a Tiger*

In Dala County, Yunan Province, there lived a peasant farmer by the name of Li Shigui whose family had worked the land for many generations.

Li owned two water buffalo, and one night when he went out to bring them in he discovered that one was missing. As he wandered among the dark fields searching for his beast, he saw an animal lying in the paddy snoring loudly. Li presumed this to be one of his missing buffalo.

He walked over and scolded the beast: "Why aren't you home yet?! It's late."

In the dim moonlight Li jumped onto the beast's back, intending to grab its horns and ride it back to the house. Only then did he realize his grave mistake.

There were ears in place of the horns he had expected, and when he looked down at the broad back onto which he had leaped, he could see the telltale orange and black stripes of a tiger. Li quickly realized that in such a situation the worst thing he could do would be to try to escape.

The tiger, rudely awakened from its slumber, leaped up with a roar and tried to shake the terrified Li off its back.

"If I jump off now, this tiger will make a meal of me," Li thought. And so he resolved to remain on the tiger's back clutching those ears with all his might. So tight was his grasp that eventually his fingers pierced the tiger's ear lobes. Still he did not release his grip. In fact he hung on even tighter.

Li's persistence drove the tiger to distraction. In anger it began bucking and weaving, leaping rivers and bounding across mountains in an effort to shake this pest from its back. In its rampaging fury the tiger's body became lacerated by thorns and prickles. This furious pace continued throughout the night until the tiger collapsed from exhaustion and died early the next morning.

Li himself was on the verge of collapse. He lay frozen, stiff as a rod, on the tiger's back, breathing only faintly.

His family had been searching for him all night, and it was in this state of near death that they finally found him. They carried the wounded man home and there the full extent of his injuries became apparent. The tiger had mauled and scratched Li's legs, exposing the bone in several places.

It was a full twelve months before he recovered from the ordeal.

# *Animals and Humans Are Equally Unpredictable*

"One should not keep a chicken for longer than three years and dogs should be gotten rid of after a maximum of six"—or so the saying goes in the *Soushenji.* Animals, it appears, should not be kept for too long.

One of my domestic servants, a man by the name of Sun Huizhong, had a big yellow dog that everyone knew to be docile and quite harmless. It had the endearing habit of begging food off the dinner table with a cheerful wag of its tail.

The dog always saw Sun off when he left on an errand and faithfully greeted him on his return home. Sun, of course, was extremely fond of his canine friend—that is, until the day the dog gouged a hole in Sun's hand as he passed down a piece of meat.

The wound was incredibly painful and poor Sun fainted from the shock and fell to the floor. Once he had recovered sufficiently, Sun beat his dog to death.

The unpredictable nature of animal behavior is similarly illustrated by the example of a tiger keeper from Yangzhou by the name of Zhao Jiu. He made his living by parading a caged tiger around the markets.

For ten coppers Zhao would let the tiger out of its cage, then place his head inside the animal's mouth and rub it between the mighty jaws until it was quite dripping with saliva. The watching crowd would roar with laughter as Zhao wandered off unharmed.

He performed this amazing stunt many times over a period of two years without mishap, until one day, while performing at Pingshan Pavilion, the tiger severed his head with one mighty bite.

The shocked crowd hurriedly notified their local officials of the disaster and a hunter was dispatched with instructions to kill the tiger.

So, because animals are regarded as unpredictable, we are often advised that humans should not live in close proximity to birds or beasts. I think this is a lot of nonsense, because human beings are equally unpredictable.

In 1746, during the reign of the Qianlong emperor, I was serving as magistrate in Jiangning County and one day I went to investigate a multiple murder in my jurisdiction. Three members of the same family had been killed—husband, wife, and child. The murderer was the wife's younger brother, a Mr. Liu.

It seemed from all my inquiries that the husband and wife had an extremely good relationship with Liu, and nobody had heard of any trouble between them.

Apparently this brother was in the habit of visiting the murdered couple's house regularly to play with his five-year-old nephew. So when her brother happened to visit on May thirteenth the young mother thought nothing of handing the boy over to her brother to look after.

However, this time Liu took the child and tossed him into a vat of water, then heaped stones on top to ensure that he would drown. When the child's mother saw what had happened she ran over in a state of shock only to be confronted with her brother wielding a knife. Liu summarily slaughtered his sister, eventually decapitating her.

Hearing his wife's screams, the husband hurried to the scene and made a vain attempt to save her. He too was savagely attacked. Liu stabbed him in the stomach, then pulled his brother-in-law's intestines out about a foot. This did not kill him immediately, and so I was able to question him about the reason for Liu's hatred.

The husband gasped with his dying breath that there had never been any problems between them.

I then asked Liu himself why he had launched such a violent attack on his sister's family. Liu gave no reply. He simply stood laughing at me while looking at the bodies out of the corner of his eye. I really couldn't understand his reasoning at all. Even so, I promptly ordered him beaten to death for his crimes.

Right up to this very day this case remains a mystery to me.

Similarly, there is the case of the widow who had maintained an unblemished record of chastity for over twenty years. Then, out of the blue, when she was well over fifty, she had an affair with a servant. She got pregnant and after a difficult labor died in childbirth.

Both of these cases show that humans are just as unpredictable as animals. They are like the tiger and the dog.

## *A Ghost Buys Herself a Son*

In Dongting there's a young scholar by the name of Ge Wenlin who has made quite a name for himself at the local college. His father's first wife, a Madam Zhou, died unexpectedly and his father remarried a Jingzhou woman, Miss Li. This was Ge Wenlin's mother.

Three days after his mother was married, she was looking through the deceased wife's wardrobe and found a red jacket embroidered with nine delicate lilies. Ge's mother fell in love with the jacket and tried it on for size.

Later that day when she went down for dinner she suddenly became delirious and began slapping herself about the face.

Then she said, "I am the first wife, Madam Zhou. I had some clothing, given to me as wedding presents, put away in a chest. I treasured these clothes too much to wear them, and now you, you who have only just married into the household, are trying to steal them from me! I won't stand for it! I'll drive you to your death. Just wait and see!"

The whole family was shocked at this outburst and immediately got onto their knees to plead for Mistress Li's life.

"Madam Zhou, what possible use do you have for such luxurious clothes now that you are dead?"

"I want to wear them now, so burn them immediately!" she replied. "It may seem sentimental and petty, but I want all the things I brought with me as part of my dowry to be burned for my use in the underworld. If you do this then I'll not harm her. I don't want that Li woman to have even one item."

The Ge family then did exactly as the ghost of the first wife had instructed and burned every single item of her dowry. The ghost then clapped her hands and said, "I'll be off now."

In an instant Li's madness disappeared.

This was a great relief to everyone in the household, but the haunting was not over yet. The next morning, while Li was putting on her cosmetics, she gave a great yawn, and in those few seconds the ghost possessed her again.

This time she said, "Get my husband over here, immediately."

Ge's father came running in and she took his hand, saying, "This new wife of yours is too young to manage the household competently. I'll come each morning to sort everything out for her."

After this, Ge's mother was possessed by the ghost of the previous wife every morning. During this time she would distribute all the grain allowances and salaries and allocate to the servants their various tasks for the day. This system worked extremely well and the household ran smoothly.

After about six months everyone was so used to this ritual that they soon forgot that the new wife was supposed to be possessed and just carried on as they normally would.

One morning Madam Zhou's ghost suddenly said to her husband: "I want to leave this house now. I've been out in the hall in this coffin long enough. Whenever someone walks by I get bumped and rattled. You know, even a ghost feels pain.

"I request that my funeral be arranged as soon as possible because only then will my soul be able to rest."

"But there are no suitable grave sites around here," her husband said.

"But there is," the wife replied. "Out to the west there's a firecracker salesman by the name of Zhang who is selling land on a hill. I went and had a look at it yesterday and I really like it. There are bamboo groves and pine trees around, so it is quite beautiful.

"Zhang says he wants sixty pieces of gold for the land but I know he'll settle for thirty-six. If you go and offer him that, I'm sure he'll sell."

Mr. Ge then went to see the patch of land, and just as she had described, it was owned by a Mr. Zhang. Seeing that his wife had been right, he immediately drew up a contract to purchase the land.

The ghost grew impatient for the funeral to be completed, but Mr. Ge had difficulties arranging it.

"Although we've got the land, the funeral invitation seems rather meager without a son's name to grace it," he explained.

"You are right, but don't worry because your new wife is now pregnant," the ghost replied. "It is not clear yet whether it is a boy or a girl, but if you give me three thousand dollars worth of ghost money, I'll buy you a son."

She then left Li's body.

When she gave birth, Mistress Li did indeed have a son, the young Wenlin. Three days after the birth, the ghost of Madam Zhou reentered Li's body and began making demands.

Mistress Li's mother-in-law, Madam Chen, scolded the ghost, saying, "Mistress Li has just given birth to her son and she's very weak. And still you harass her! How can you be so heartless?"

The reply came: "You're wrong to scold me. I bought this son for her with my ghost money and in the future he will reciprocate and make offerings to my spirit. Our bond will last forever.

"This new mother is young and needs her sleep. She could easily squash the baby if she happened to fall asleep while feeding him. Madam Chen, you should take the baby away after she has breast-fed him. He can sleep with you in between feedings. Only then will I be free of worries."

Madam Chen promptly agreed to this routine. Mistress Li then gave a big yawn and the ghost left her body.

The arrival of a son meant that the funeral preparations could begin in earnest. Mr. Ge, busy arranging the coarse hempen mourning clothes for the immediate family to wear, decided the baby should have a finer hemp since it was only a month old.

The ghost of Madam Zhou then spoke out: "All direct descendants of the deceased should wear the coarser cloth. He is my son, so he must wear the appropriate weight of cloth to his mother's funeral."

Ge dutifully put the baby into the rough hempen cloth.

Just before the coffin was lowered into the ground, Mistress Li was again possessed by Zhou's spirit.

"My spirit has found peace at last. I will go now and never return!" she cried.

As expected, the ghost of Madam Zhou never again appeared in the Ge household.

It is said that when Madam Zhou was a young girl in her native village, she was an extremely close friend to two other girls. The three of them swore to live together and die together. The other two sisters had just died when Madam Zhou grew sick.

During her illness she said to her husband, "My sisters have come for me! There they are, beckoning to me from the foot of the bed!"

Mr. Ge was livid. He ran for his sword and started slashing and stabbing wildly at the ghosts.

Madam Zhou then became angry and stamped her feet. "You could have tried a bit of gentle persuasion!" she shouted. "But no, you just rush ahead and now you've cut off their arms! I'm certain to die now!"

Surely enough, she collapsed and died as soon as she had finished speaking. She was only twenty-three years old.

## *Poor Ghosts Haunt, Rich Ghosts Don't Bother*

In the West Lake region is the Desheng nunnery. Stacked high outside the back door of the nunnery are hundreds of coffins. I stayed there for a while on my travels and when I asked a nun if they had ever been troubled by ghosts, she said, "No, it's peaceful here because all the ghosts in this area are quite wealthy."

I was rather puzzled by this reply and asked, "There can't possibly be so many rich people in this region. How can you have such rich ghosts when there aren't so many rich people? Besides, these coffins are just stacked here, still unburied, so they can't possibly be from rich families."

The nun replied, "When I said they were rich I didn't mean that they were rich when they were alive. They are rich ghosts because they have plenty of offerings and ghost money burned for them now that they are dead.

"It is true that we have over a thousand coffins stored here unburied, but we nuns are vigilant about observing the correct rituals and making generous offerings all year round.

"We have a huge ceremony on the fifteenth of July for Ghost Festival day. Thousands and thousands in ghost money are burned on that one day. We also make sure there is plenty of food and drink available, because if the ghosts are well fed they have no reason to harbor resentment against anyone.

"You must have noticed, sir, that whenever there is crime—cheating or robbery, for instance—there is hunger. Have you also not observed that sick people often see ghosts and describe them as being well dressed and well fed? The ghosts that haunt people are the poverty-stricken ones with disheveled hair, rotten, jutting teeth, and torn clothes."

The nun's explanation seemed plausible to me, and sure enough, although I stayed there with quite a number of my servants for over a month, none of us heard any ghostly, ghoulish noises during the night.

# *Revenge of the Wronged Wife*

In Hangzhou a coppersmith by the name of Xu Songnian opened a store in the wealthy suburb of Xianlin Bridge. When he was only thirty-two years old he suddenly became extremely ill. His sickness grew worse and worse and everyone fully expected him to die.

His wife cried and cried, saying, "We have two young sons. How will I manage if you die? I'm going to pray to the gods to exchange my life for yours.

"You would then be able to raise our sons to be good husbands and fathers themselves. The family line will thus continue without your having to remarry."

Xu agreed to her plan and so the wife went to the city god's temple to say her prayer. Then she returned home to pray to her husband's ancestors, so that they would be aware of the exchange she hoped would occur.

Surely enough, she grew sicker and sicker as her husband grew stronger and stronger. Within the year she had died. It wasn't long after her death that Songnian remarried, having forgotten his promise.

On their wedding night Songnian and his new wife, Mistress Cao, found themselves unable to consummate their union—a cold body lay on the bed between them. The bride leaped up in terror and in the light of the candle they saw lying on the bed the maid of Xu's former wife. Clearly possessed, her mouth moving mechanically, she heaped a torrent of abuse upon them.

The newlyweds slept like this for four or five months, having failed to placate the ghost with prayers and offerings. Xu Songnian died soon after this.

# *A Ghost Makes an Offering of Dumplings*

Mr. Zhong of Hengtang, Hangzhou, employed a private tutor by the name of Wang Shengyu. Mr. Zhong's third son, Zhong Youtiao, was twenty years old, but he decided to trick his tutor and pretend to be only sixteen.

He asked Scholar Wang if it was all right for him to study even though he was only sixteen, and was given the reply that age was of no consequence; it was the degree of determination that mattered.

Youtiao thought this an astute answer and so he worked diligently at his studies from then on.

Zhong's father was the sort of merchant who wasn't keen on having his son spend all his time studying, so he insisted that Youtiao make regular business trips to Wumen. Youtiao was very unhappy about this, but he complied with his father's wishes all the same.

During the day he would work in the markets and in the evening he would rush home to catch up on his studies, working late into the night and often hiding in seclusion behind his bed curtains. The walls of his room were plastered with posters bearing words to the effect that "life has not been kind to me."

After four months of this busy life he became very ill, and on returning home one night, just before the Double Ninth Festival, he collapsed and died. His bereaved family placed his coffin in the main hall.

The next year, on the night of July seventh, Scholar Wang was awakened by the sound of his study door opening. A figure made its way towards his bed, and when Wang raised his bed curtains he saw it was his old pupil Youtiao. Youtiao walked towards him with a candle in his left hand and a steaming bowl of food in his right.

As he reached Wang's bed he said with a smile: "Teacher, you must be hungry, so I've prepared a small dish especially for you."

Scholar Wang accepted the proffered bowl and saw that it held four dumplings and a copper spoon.

He automatically began to eat, unmindful of the fact that he had been given the food by a ghost. He ate three of the dumplings and was quite full, so he handed the bowl with the remaining dumpling back to Youtiao.

Youtiao promptly lowered the bed curtains and walked out of the room. It was only then that Scholar Wang realized the full significance of what had just taken place.

"Youtiao has been dead for nearly a year, so how could he possibly have been here tonight?"

When he realized it must have been Youtiao's ghost, a cold chill rose through his body. He spent the remainder of the night running back and forth to the toilet with diarrhea. By morning he was thoroughly exhausted, so he asked his employers if he could return to his family home while he recovered.

Arriving home, he found his doorway blocked by a countless variety of ghosts. There were male and female ghosts, big and small ghosts, local ghosts and ghosts from distant lands. Some were in the shape of turtledoves, others wore the tattered clothing of the poverty-stricken. Fortunately, although they were all rather strange, none was really frightening or horrible.

Scholar Wang's younger sister had married into the Zhai family, and when she came home to visit her sick brother a ghost said through Wang's mouth, "You are Madam Zhai of Zhengjia Bridge. Have you also come to visit me?"

When Wang's younger brother later went to Zhengjia Bridge he heard that his sister's neighbor, the barber's wife, had just hung herself.

A doctor was called for Wang, but when the prescription had been prepared, the ghosts crowded round, pinned Wang's arms, and blocked his mouth so that he couldn't take the medicine.

This went on for quite a while until eventually Scholar Wang abandoned the struggle. He had no choice but to ignore his father's orders that he swallow the medicine.

The next morning a second doctor was summoned and asked to check the previous prescription. The doctor examined the script and said to Wang's father in a startled voice, "Lucky he didn't take this medicine—it would certainly have been his last drink!"

He wrote another prescription, and when the time came for Wang to drink the medicine he wasn't harassed by the ghosts.

For ten days after this the house was filled with so many ghosts that they blocked the sunlight during the day and swamped the lamplight at night. They would stand around laughing and chatting. The terrified Wang family chanted sutras and said prayers in the hope that the ghost inhabiting the scholar's body would leave, but to no avail.

One day a female ghost called out, "You should invite the old monk Hongdao here. Then we'll leave you in peace."

The family arranged for Hongdao to visit, and as soon as he arrived on the doorstep the ghosts and the illness disappeared.

Master Yuan Mai commented on this incident, saying one can never be certain which sutras will work with which ghost. People must deal with ghosts on an individual basis and not try to apply one hard-and-fast rule to all of them. He also said that everyone should know that some food is suitable only for ghostly consumption and that Youtiao's offering to his human teacher reflected a stupid and ignorant form of loyalty and filial piety.

# *You Don't Have to Be Virtuous to Become a God*

One autumn a scholar by the name of Li Haizhong made his way to the capital to sit the national examinations. Upon reaching Suzhou, he hired a boat to travel up the River Huai.

As he was standing at the stern, a man on the bank waved to him and asked if he could hitch a ride. Recognizing the man to be an old neighbor, a Mr. Wang, Li didn't see any reason to refuse, so he invited him on board.

That evening as they were moored along the riverbank Wang asked Li with a little laugh, "Are you a courageous sort of person?"

Scholar Li was a bit surprised by this question, but he calmly replied, "Yes, I consider myself a man of courage."

Wang then explained, "I was a little worried you might be fainthearted, and I wanted to reassure myself that this wasn't the case before I told you that I am a ghost and not a man.

"Since you are a brave sort, it's all right to tell you. We haven't seen each other for six years or so, you'll recall.

"Last year a famine swept our region and I resorted to robbing graves to survive. I was apprehended by the police, tried in court, and sentenced to immediate execution. Even though I am now a ghost I'm still living a life of hunger, so I have decided to go to the capital to reclaim a debt. Luckily I ran into you. Would you help me get there?"

"Who's in debt to you?" Li asked.

"An official at the Board of Punishment by the name of Wang," came the reply. "When he was processing my execution documents I gave him five hundred pieces of gold in the hope that he could reduce my sentence. How was I to know that he would just pocket the money and leave me to die? I've decided to get my revenge by haunting him."

Li was shocked at this revelation because the official in question was a relative of his, and so he said, "You committed a crime that is punishable by death, so the Board of Punishment passed a just sentence. However, this relative of mine should never have accepted the bribe from you.

"Why don't you come with me to see him and we'll try to get your money back and resolve this case once and for all. But what possible use would you have for the money now that you're dead?"

"Although I myself would have no use for it, my wife and children would be very grateful for such a sum. When it is repaid can I entrust you to take it to them for me?" the ghost replied.

Li agreed to this request and they continued on their way.

Several days later they arrived at the outskirts of the capital. Wang then told Li to go on to his relative's alone, saying, "This relative of yours is a miserly fellow, and I suspect that if we just go and talk it over with him, he'll refuse to hand over the money.

"What I propose to do is haunt him and his family for a while, and when they've failed to exorcize me from their house you can come along and explain the situation to him. They might be more inclined to believe you then."

Having explained his plan, Wang the ghost disappeared.

Scholar Li then went into the city alone. He found some lodgings and waited three days before going to see his relative.

When he reached the house he was told that his relative had been struck by a disease that rendered its victims quite insane. The ailing man's family had called in a fortuneteller and then a spirit medium, but neither had been able to do anything for the man.

As soon as Li walked in the door of the sickroom, however, the ailing man yelled out, "My savior has arrived at last!"

Li was greeted enthusiastically by Wang's family, who quizzed him about the meaning of the invalid's outburst. Li then told them the tale of bribery and explained how the debt could be paid.

Wang's wife suggested that they repay the debt with ghost money and was quite prepared to burn millions of taels' worth.

The sick man just laughed out loud, saying, "What sort of a deal is that? Repaying a debt of real money with fake money? No deal is that simple in the business world! Hurry up and give Mr. Li the five hundred gold pieces that you owe me. Then I'll leave you in peace."

Seeing that there was no choice in the matter, Wang's wife handed over the money. As promised, the illness then disappeared.

A few days passed and then Li was visited in his lodgings by the ghost, who wanted Li to begin the journey back to his widow and children immediately.

Li refused, explaining, "I haven't sat my examinations yet."

The ghost then said knowingly, "You're going to fail, so why bother?"

Li didn't believe him and carried on with his preparations. When he had completed all three sessions the ghost returned and began pestering him to leave. Li refused again. "I want to wait for the results."

"What's the point in waiting for the results? You're going to fail anyway!" the ghost replied.

When the results were eventually posted, Li had indeed failed.

"Now are you ready to leave?" the ghost teased him.

Li was depressed and also a little embarrassed, but he nevertheless made a start that very day.

Together again, they departed on their boat journey. Li noticed that the ghost never ate anything but did enjoy smelling food. As soon as he had sniffed at it, the food turned cold.

They stopped at a town along the river and took lodgings together. The ghost told Li there was an opera he was keen to see, so Li went with him and the two of them stood right up close to the stage.

After a few acts the ghost suddenly disappeared. When Li turned to look for him a huge gust of wind blew up, throwing rocks and sand across the audience. It was nearly dark when Li returned alone to the boat.

When the ghost finally appeared he was dressed in expensive clothes. He explained his transformation thus: "I won't be returning with you. I have been asked to stay here and be the god of war, Guandi."

Li was absolutely scandalized. "How dare you pose as Guandi?"

The ghost replied, "All the Guandis and goddesses of mercy that you see around you are ghostly imposters. The townsfolk were holding that opera to thank their particular Guandi, but that guy is nowhere near as worthy as me!

"I got really angry at the thought of this worthless fellow holding such a position, so I decided to pick a fight with him. I've chased him off now, well and truly. Didn't you notice all those stones being blown up?"

He then thanked Li for his help and bade him farewell.

Li continued on to the ghost's village and gave his widow and children the five hundred gold pieces.

# *In Which the Ghost Sues Her Loved One*

In Zhenjiang there was a young man by the name of Bao who was most handsome and, some thought, sexually attractive in the extreme. He married a young woman from the Wang family, but because he had succeeded to a long line of merchants, he was often away on business or out entertaining customers and friends.

In the autumn of 1780 Bao and several of his friends went carousing in the red-light district. They progressed from brothel to brothel and it was extremely late by the time Bao set out for home.

Mistress Wang was in her kitchen with an old serving woman preparing dinner when there was a knock at the door. She asked the servant to answer it, and when the door was opened the servant saw a well-dressed, heavily made-up young woman. The old woman asked her name but received no reply. Deciding this silent visitor must be a relative, she welcomed her in and went to tell her mistress.

Mistress Wang hurried to the front room to greet the mysterious visitor but found only her husband, Bao, sitting there. She laughed at the old woman for her silly mistake, but stopped short when she noticed that Bao's mannerisms were those of a woman.

The visitor stood up and said with grace and due decorum, "Your husband, Mr. Bao, was drinking at a brothel. I waited outside and came home with him."

Wang examined the performance closely—the body was Bao's but the voice and mannerisms were not his at all.

Her first thought was that Bao had gone insane, so she called for the houseboys and sent them to fetch the rest of the family. They all gathered in the front room and the visitor greeted each of them very politely and with the utmost propriety—but adopting the manners and form usually reserved for aristocratic women.

Some of the men had a great laugh at this and made a few indecent proposals and rude gestures to the feminized Bao.

The ghost within Bao responded angrily, "I am a virtuous woman. Come near me and I'll kill you!"

Perplexed by this sudden change, the family asked what grievance she had against Bao.

She replied in a calmer voice, "The hostility that has been generated between Mr. Bao and myself has romantic origins. I have lodged nineteen separate complaints against him with the city god for failing to reciprocate my love. I have had no satisfaction with that course so now I've lodged a complaint at Lord Dongyue's temple.

"Lord Dongyue has finally given me the opportunity for an official hearing, so Bao and I will go and resolve the case during the next few days."

They asked for her name but the ghost replied, "I am from a good family and I will not release my name."

Someone else then asked, "What charges are you laying?"

The ghost then listed nineteen separate offenses, but did so very quickly, and so nobody was really sure of the details.

Basically, she wanted Bao prosecuted for not returning her love and thereby causing her to be a homeless, drifting ghost.

The next question was, "Now that you're in Bao's body, where is his soul?"

She smiled. "I've tied him up and locked him in the little room next to the city god's temple."

This was all too much for Bao's wife. She dropped to her knees and entreated the ghost to release her husband, but her pleas were ignored.

Later that night a few of the relatives discussed the matter. One of them said, "The ghost told us that she'd had no luck filing her complaint with the city god, and yet she's locked Bao up near his temple. How about if we go and explain the whole problem to the city god? He might be able to make sure that justice is carried out."

Thus decided, they gathered together the necessary candles and incense, but just as they were about to step out the door the ghost appeared from nowhere and confronted them: "You're going to get help from the city god, aren't you? Don't bother, I'll release Bao now and we'll let Lord Dongyue give his verdict."

In an instant, Bao collapsed in a heap on the floor. It wasn't long before he regained consciousness, complaining of unbearable exhaustion. Everyone bustled around, interrogating him about the strange incident.

Bao related the course of events as follows: "When I left the brothel

I saw this woman following me and I grew increasingly suspicious when after some time she was still there. Just as we came to the courtyard outside the Academy, she rushed forward and pushed me into a small room just to the left of the city god's temple. My arms and legs were bound and I was tossed in a heap on the floor.

"It appeared that I was not alone, for even though I saw nobody, I felt that I was being guarded. Next thing I knew, the woman had returned to tell me she would let me go.

"She pushed me out the door and I tripped and fell. Now I'm here! As far as I know, it's all going to be sorted out tomorrow by Lord Dongyue."

This wasn't a sufficient explanation for his anxious relatives, but their questions went unheeded because Bao promptly fell into a deep sleep. When he woke late in the afternoon of the following day, his first instructions were to have a feast prepared for the legal officers that had arrived. He then went into the front hall and bowed and gestured as if he was welcoming guests.

Although he said quite a few things, nothing was comprehensible to the astonished family that had gathered around him.

After the feast was laid out Bao went back to bed. Around the first watch of the evening he passed away, but because his chest was still slightly warm, Mistress Wang and other close family members kept a constant vigil over the body.

During the night his face changed color several times. It was sometimes blue, sometimes yellow, and sometimes red. There was no obvious pattern to the color changes. Around the third watch, they noticed red scratches on his chest, cheeks, and throat.

The next night, around the second watch, his hair became disheveled and lost its texture.

Towards dawn of the third day he woke up and demanded rice and tea. He gobbled down more than ten bowls of rice and numerous pots of tea at such a pace that his watching relatives grew frightened. However, his general state improved after this tremendous meal and he then gave detailed instructions to those around him. More wine and food was to be prepared by Mistress Wang herself for the officers from the underworld who accompanied him.

Six thousand cash in ghost money was to be burned, but they had to make sure that none of the notes were crumpled or torn. Four thousand of these were to be burned in front of the lounge and the remaining two thousand in the lane that ran along the side entrance to the house.

Bao himself then rose and went to the gate, bowing repeatedly and gesturing like one who was seeing off guests. He then returned to his bed and slept for two days.

After this rest he was able to tell his family what had happened. In the afternoon of the day after the ghost had released him, two officers of the law from the underworld had come to fetch him. He recognized one of them as a former classmate, Merchant Chen's young son who had died three years earlier, but the other officer was a stranger.

The Chen family were quite poor, so when it came time for this young fellow to marry, Bao had helped out by giving him a few thousand cash.

Chen said to Bao, "Your case is currently before the court, so it has certainly been investigated. Don't worry, though. We've been friends a long time now, and I have not forgotten your past kindness. I'll not put the cangue and chains on you."

On their way to the courtroom they passed two other officers who were guarding the chained ghost. Writhing in anger, she butted Bao and then scratched his face—hence the marks on Bao's body. She cursed the officers and demanded to know why Bao wasn't chained, so Bao was duly restrained.

They walked for what seemed an eternity into darker and darker regions where a fierce, cold wind tossed Bao's hair wildly. Finally they arrived at a place that looked rather like a courtroom and here both prisoners were told to sit on the ground and wait.

The light of two red lanterns could be seen moving towards them from within the building, and at this signal the officers came forward and removed Bao's chains. He was ordered to kneel at a spot just before the lanterns.

Then Bao saw the magistrate's bench, piled with documents. Behind it sat an official wearing a gown of red and black gauze.

As the magistrate smoothed his beard he asked, "Are you Bao?"

Bao replied in the affirmative and then the ghost was summoned.

She also knelt on the steps in front of the bench and answered a variety of questions, but although Bao was only about a foot away, he couldn't hear a word. He could see, however, that at one point the magistrate became extremely angry and ordered one of the officers to slap the ghost about the face fifteen times or so.

She then had her chains put back on and was dragged back crying and weeping by the two officers.

At this point, Bao was still on his knees in front of the bench. It was as if he were kneeling in mud. The cold was unbearable, and whenever the chilly wind picked up and blew across his face, he felt as if he were being stabbed by knives.

As the ghost was being slapped, Officer Chen leaned down and whispered to him, "You have won the case. I'll tidy up your hair for you."

*Court Scene from the Underworld*

When Bao lifted his head again, the lanterns, the bench, and the magistrate had all disappeared. The two remaining officers told him he could return home, but reminded him that he owed four thousand cash to the officers for their efforts and that it was appropriate to make a personal gift to Chen of two thousand cash.

Everyone was puzzled about the identity of the woman, whom Bao insisted he had never seen before. She was a complete stranger who had died from unrequited love for the famously handsome Bao. When she became a ghost she decided to fabricate charges with the intention of dragging Bao down to the underworld to be her partner in death.

Fortunately, her harebrained scheme was discovered by the magistrate of the underworld and she received her due punishment.

# *Elder Brother Ding*

During the reign of the Kangxi emperor, a peasant farmer from the Yangzhou region by the name of Second Brother Yu went into town to pick up the cash he'd earned from the sale of his recent wheat crop. The purchaser insisted he stay on for a few pots of wine, and by the time Yu set off for home it was late and the road was pitch black.

As he approached Red Bridge he was jumped by more than a dozen dwarflike ghosts, who clung tightly to his clothing. Yu knew ghosts were rampant in the area but he was a tough and fearless sort of man and besides he was emboldened by the wine. So he fought hard against these ghosts, vigorously brandishing his fists. But no sooner had he fought off one bunch than another formed to attack him.

In the midst of the fray Second Brother Yu overheard one of the ghosts say, "This guy's too tough for us. There's no way we can beat him. Let's get Elder Brother Ding. I bet he'd be able to put this guy away."

The ghosts ran off noisily and Yu was left alone to ponder the horror of Elder Brother Ding. Eventually he decided, in a rather fatalistic frame of mind, that since he had come this far he would keep going and deal with whatever came for him when it arrived.

Indeed, he had only just crossed Red Bridge when he was confronted by a ghost of enormous proportions. It was over ten feet tall, and in the shadowy light Yu could just make out the green and purple colors of his face. All in all it was a sinister, terrifying sight.

Yu knew that his only possibility of success was to take the initiative straightaway. His best chance was to strike before the ghost expected it, so he untied his money belt, filled as it was with the two thousand coppers he'd received earlier in the day, and hurled it with all his might at his opponent.

The ghost fell instantaneously to the ground, making a clinking sound as it hit the stone paving. Yu ran over and trampled the ghost beneath his boots, and although it never became any lighter, it gradually shrank.

Holding its diminished form tightly, Yu returned home. Under the candlelight he saw that the ghost was actually a big iron nail—the type that had been used in old-style coffins. It was over two feet long and shaped like a huge thumb. To kill the ghost Yu burned the nail, and blood oozed from the flames.

Later when Yu was telling his friends about his ordeal he boasted jokingly, "Elder Brother Ding was no match for the strength of Second Brother Yu."

# *Miss Wang Er*

In the Department of Justice within the Zhaozhou provincial government there worked a scribe by the name of Wu. Now Wu was the third son in his family and was originally from Shaoxing.

After a while another scribe was employed and coincidentally he was the third son born to another Wu family. However, he was originally from Suzhou.

To avoid confusion, the people in the office called them Old Master Wu and Young Master Wu. The two Master Wus were quite good friends. Both men lived in the government dormitory and had rooms directly across the hall from each other.

The governor at that time had seven or eight concubines and numerous maids, all of whom were exceptionally beautiful, and the Wus had often seen them strolling near the dormitory. So captivating were these women that the men would often joke about the possibility of secret trysts, which woman each would prefer, and the like. It was, however, all empty talk.

One night they worked late, getting back to their rooms only around the third watch. Young Wu sat down on the edge of his bed and smoked a cigarette. He then lit the candles on the table outside the bed curtains and asked his manservant to leave so he could go to sleep.

The entire magistry was quiet until someone pushed open the door to Wu's room and walked in. Young Master Wu asked who it was but received no reply.

He peered through the darkness and saw an exceptionally beautiful young woman of about twenty walking quickly towards him. She stopped at the edge of the bed and stared down at him.

Young Master Wu was terrified and asked, "Who are you? What are you doing here?"

The woman replied, "I am Miss Wang Er and I have come to find

Third Master Wu from Shaoxing. It looks as though I have come to the wrong place."

Young Wu assumed that Miss Wang Er must be a maid sent by the boss to keep Old Wu company for the night, so he laughed and pointed across the hall. "Third Master Wu from Shaoxing lives in the room opposite. I'm Third Master Wu from Suzhou."

The woman turned and left.

The next morning Young Wu teased his friend. "Did you have fun last night?"

Old Wu looked perplexed and asked what he meant. So Young Wu mentioned the young woman. But when Old Wu kept asking more questions he said impatiently, "I saw her with my own eyes! How can you deny it?"

Old Wu then grew increasingly anxious and persisted with his questions. Young Wu described Miss Wang Er's clothes and appearance, then explained how she had specifically asked for Third Master Wu from Shaoxing.

The color suddenly drained from Old Wu's face and he said in a panic, "Why has she come here?"

After a while, when he had calmed down sufficiently, he explained to Young Wu, "She is a close relative of mine but she's been dead for over a decade. I have no idea why she has come looking for me now."

Young Wu was startled by the explanation and was about to question his friend further when he noticed that Old Wu's depressed face was filled with despair. So he decided not to press him.

That night as time for sleep drew nearer, Old Wu became increasingly silent and his fear became more and more obvious to those around him. He begged Young Wu to sleep in his room, but Young Wu did not relish this prospect and refused. Old Wu then ordered his two servants to sleep on either side of his bed.

All that night Young Wu listened for any sound from across the hall, but heard nothing strange. The next morning, however, the two servants woke to find Old Wu dead.

# *Double Blossom Temple*

In Guilin, during the reign of the Yongzheng emperor, there lived a fashionable young scholar by the name of Cai who was extremely good-looking.

One day, as he was standing in the theater watching a troupe of actors perform, he felt someone brush up against him and stroke his buttocks. He turned intending to strike his assailant, but stopped in his tracks when he saw a young man even better-looking than himself. His heart melted and he began to gently stroke the other man's penis in return.

Overjoyed at this mutual affection, the young man and Scholar Cai straightened their clothes in preparation for a more formal exchange of names. It turned out the young man was also from a wealthy Guilin family, and although he had not yet been formally admitted to a college, he too was an aspiring scholar.

They walked hand in hand to a restaurant called Apricot Blossom Village, and after drinking heavily they swore undying loyalty to each other. From this point on the two young men were inseparable—they always traveled in the same carriage, ate together, and slept together.

It wasn't long before they began imitating female fashions—wearing perfume, shaving their faces, and donning short-sleeved gowns. In fact, strangers would not have known whether they were male or female.

Unfortunately the town bully, a fellow known by the name of Wang Tuer, decided to rape these two young men. He hid in an isolated spot on the outskirts of town and pounced when the pair walked by. They both tried to struggle free but in the course of the fight were killed. Wang then dumped their bodies in the shade of an isolated section of the city wall.

The parents of the murdered young men lodged a complaint with the local magistrate and in the ensuing investigation Wang was charged with the murders. Traces of blood had been found on his clothing by the investigating police, so he confessed to the crime and was summarily executed.

The two young men had been well liked by all the townsfolk who knew them. They had been admired for their intelligence, breadth of knowledge, polite manners, and general good behavior. The locals, saddened by their deaths, decided to build a temple in their honor. Worshipers often brought apricot blossoms to place on the altar and so the temple assumed the name Double Blossom Temple.

The townsfolk's kindness did not go unrewarded, for the prayers of the worshipers were always answered. As the reputation of the temple spread, it became more and more popular and the offerings and incense increased accordingly.

This happy state of affairs continued for some years until one day the county magistrate, Liu, happened to pass by and inquire about the origins of Double Blossom Temple. When he found out the history of the temple he became extremely angry and declared, "This is a temple of depravity! Why should we worship two such obscene young men?!" He immediately instructed the local constable to raze the temple.

That night Magistrate Liu dreamed that two young men came to his room. The first grabbed his beard and the second spat in his face and cursed him. "How would you know whether we were obscene or not! You never met us and you certainly were no friend of ours. You're just a civil servant from a distant office, so you certainly wouldn't have any idea of what we did between the sheets.

"During the Three Kingdoms Period the handsome young pair Zhou Yu and Sun Ce lived together, ate together, and slept together and yet everyone today recognizes them as heroes! Are you going to say that they too are obscene?

"In your position as magistrate you have taken bribes in every case under your control, and one year you even had Scholar Zhou executed on very flimsy grounds.

"It is you who are truly wicked! How dare you judge us to be obscene?! We were planning on taking your life tonight but we've since found that the police are onto you and your death is imminent, so we'll let you off this time."

One of the young men then drew a stick about three feet long from his sleeves. He twisted the magistrate's hair tightly around the stick, then proclaimed, "When your time comes you'll understand the significance of this gesture."

Liu woke with a fright and told his family about his dream. He ordered the temple rebuilt but was too ashamed to publicize the reason for his change in policy.

However, not long after this he was charged with accepting bribes and sentenced to death by strangulation. Only then did he understand the stick's significance.

# *The Female Impersonator*

In Guiyang County there lived an extremely beautiful man by the name of Hong. He made a living teaching embroidery to young women by posing as a traveling female embroidery tutor in Hunan and Guizhou provinces.

One year he was employed in Changsha by a scholar named Li. Now Li, who believed Hong to be a young woman, planned to seduce his new employee. But when he approached Hong, the latter confessed to being a man.

Scholar Li laughed and said, "It's even better if you're a man! I have always thought that the tale of the female impersonators of the Northern Wei was a great tragedy.

"The ruler of Wei visited his mother, the empress dowager, in the palace and saw two beautiful nuns in attendance. He summoned them to his rooms with the intention of having his way with them only to discover they were men. The extremely foolish ruler of Wei then ordered that they be summarily executed.

"Why didn't he take these two on as his personal bum-boys in his own Longyang palace? If he'd done this he would have won the loyalty of these servants and avoided offending the empress dowager."

Hong understood what was being asked and agreed. Scholar Li was very kind and cherished Hong as a lover should.

A few years later Hong traveled to Jiangxia, where a man by the name of Du, also assuming Hong to be a woman, tried to seduce him. Hong hoped that Du would be as kind as Scholar Li, so he flirted charmingly, anticipating a generous reaction. Unfortunately, Du was not as accommodating and instead dragged Hong off to the police to have him prosecuted.

After the arrest Hong was deported to Guiyang, where he was given a physical examination by the police inspector. The inspector found that Hong lacked an Adam's apple and as a consequence had a soft, delicate voice.

Moreover, Hong's hair was so long that when it was untied it reached the ground. His skin was as smooth as silk and his waist measured a tiny twenty inches.

His penis, however, was thick and firm and shaped like a large mushroom.

Hong explained in his confession that he was orphaned as a young child and had been raised by a widowed neighbor. The widow and he had an affair that lasted many years. To avoid scandal he had grown his hair long, bound his feet, and lived as a woman. The widow died when he was seventeen, whereupon he began his life as a wandering seamstress teaching embroidery.

Hong was now twenty-seven and had lost count of the number of women with whom he had had liaisons in his ten-odd years of living as a female.

The inspector demanded a list of the names of the women but Hong replied, "Isn't it enough to punish me? Why punish the daughters of respected families as well?"

This response was deemed quite unsatisfactory, so the inspector tormented Hong with the cruelest of tortures in an attempt to force him to release their names.

The provincial governor heard of the case and recommended that the imposter be exiled, but the police inspector insisted that because Hong was such a bewitching transvestite he deserved an extreme punishment. Indeed the inspector recommended execution.

The day before the sentence was due to be carried out Hong said to his jailers, "I have enjoyed pleasures that most men only dream of, so I have no regrets as I go to my death. But, you know, this inspector won't come away clean from this case.

"At worst my crimes are those of illicit sexual relations and of seduction by pretending to be a woman. Mine is simply a case of seduction, and there are no laws that advocate the death sentence for such a crime.

"Moreover, my illicit affairs with these various women should not be made public. If you force me to give you their names, then many women across dozens of counties will face corporal punishment.

"Many girls from good families will be caned and their silky smooth white skin will be beaten to a red leathery bark."

The next day he was led to the market square to face the executioner. As he knelt on the ground he said, "Three years from now the man who passed this sentence will end up here too." Surely enough, in three years the inspector was indeed executed. The accuracy of Hong's prediction caused quite a stir among the locals.

A similar case of female impersonation was noted in the dynastic records during the Jiajing reign of the Ming dynasty. A transvestite by the name of San Chong lived a similar life and faced an identical death. It is a mystery that San Chong didn't seek revenge on his judge, as Hong had.

# *Tools of the Sex Trade*

The third son of one of the junior secretaries at the Board of Revenue, surnamed Jiang, considered himself to be quite a sensual sort of fellow and an accomplished womanizer. One day as he was strolling near the Haidai Gate he saw a beautiful woman sitting in a carriage.

She saw him looking at her and didn't appear to take offense until he started following the carriage. She then grew angry at his impertinence, but when he persisted her anger turned to mirth and she gave him a wave.

Jiang was thrilled to have this positive reaction so he continued following the carriage. Every now and then the woman would turn back to look at Jiang as if she too was interested in a liaison.

Jiang was soon beside himself with anticipation and before he knew it his legs had carried him a distance of seven or eight miles.

Eventually the carriage stopped outside a large house and the woman went inside. Jiang, feeling rather foolish, stood dithering outside for a while. He didn't dare go in, but at the same time, he didn't want to leave when he'd come so close to realizing his fantasy.

As he paced back and forth trying to come to a decision, a young maidservant waved to him and then pointed in the direction of a small door along the side of the house.

Jiang took the hint and went in through the door only to find that it was just a toilet. The maid then whispered to Jiang that he should wait for a while. Jiang stood in the toilet and endured the suffocating stench.

Precisely at dusk the maid opened the door and led him through the house. They passed by the kitchen and various other rooms and eventually arrived at the entrance to the main hall of the residence. The doorway was decorated in luxurious style and hung with vermilion drapes, beside which stood two houseboys.

Jiang was feeling rather pleased with himself. It was as if he had entered a kingdom of angels. He straightened his clothes and patted down his hair and went into the hall. At the southern end of the hall a large man with a thick black beard sat crosslegged on a brick bed, leaning back against a pillow. The hairs on his legs were as thick as the spines of a hedgehog.

The man shouted angrily at Jiang, "Who are you?! Why have you come here?!"

Jiang was so terrified that his whole body shook and quite unconsciously he dropped to his knees. Before he had time to answer he heard the rattle of jade bracelets, and there entering the room was the woman from the carriage.

The bearded man sat her on his knee and said to Jiang, "This is Zhutuan, my beautiful and treasured concubine. Your interest in her shows that at least you have good taste. But everything has an owner. You must be an idiot to think you could taste the meat of a dragon from heaven!"

He then began to kiss the concubine and fondle her breasts, deliberately taunting the young Jiang.

Jiang, helplessly embarrassed, kowtowed and requested permission to leave.

The bearded man said, "You must have been very interested to have come all this way. How can you leave without first satisfying your curiosity?"

He then asked Jiang about his parents, and Jiang answered quite honestly.

The bearded man replied, "What a reckless fellow you are! Your father was a colleague of mine so you are practically a nephew to me. How dare a nephew lust after his uncle's concubine?! What sort of disgusting behavior is that?!"

He then ordered his attendants to bring out a large stick and said, "I will teach my friend's son a lesson he will never forget."

An attendant returned with a huge pole and another pushed Jiang's head to the floor, ripped off his pants, and exposed his buttocks. Jiang wept and pleaded for mercy and eventually the concubine climbed off the bed and knelt down in front of her master.

"Please have mercy on him," she said to the bearded man. "His buttocks are even softer and whiter than mine! I don't think I could bear to see them beaten. Why don't you just treat him as a male concubine and sodomize him? He could probably cope with that."

"Sodomize the son of a friend of mine! I couldn't do that!" the bearded man retorted.

So the woman made another suggestion: "Everyone who comes to worship at a temple brings an offering. He has come to us with a specific deed in mind so he must have brought a tool of trade. Let's have a look at it."

So the bearded man ordered his two attendants to examine Jiang's penis. After delving around in Jiang's clothing for a while they reported, "It is as small as a silkworm and the foreskin has not yet retracted."

Stroking his bearded chin, the man bellowed, "Shame on you! Trying to knock off other people's women with such a pitiful tool! Huh!"

He then tossed a small knife onto the floor and said to the attendants, "This young fellow loves sex, so why don't you two fix up his sex tool for him!"

One of the attendants picked up the knife, grabbed Jiang's penis, and made as if to cut the foreskin. By this stage Jiang's face was awash in tears and mucus.

The concubine, her cheeks flushed, climbed down from the bed and spoke once more. "My lord, you've gone far enough. Any more and I would be embarrassed. Our donkey is sick and I would love to have some dumplings for dinner tonight. Although we have ample grain we still need someone to pull the grindstone. Why don't you make him replace the donkey and grind the wheat for us?"

The bearded man asked if Jiang was prepared to perform this task and the young man, lacking an alternative, promptly assented.

The concubine then embraced her master and the two of them lay back against the pillows while the attendants brought the grindstone and the wheat to a position just outside one of the nearby windows. Jiang was ordered to begin grinding and the attendants showered his back with lashes from their whips, just as if they were spurring on a donkey.

Jiang pulled the grindstone all night long, and the next morning he heard the man say, "He's had enough! Give him a dumpling and let him leave through the dogs' door!"

Jiang was bedridden for a month after this incident.

# *Stealing Ginseng*

One of the larger ginseng stores in the capital is the Zhang Guang. One day a young man tethered his horse outside and wandered in to buy some ginseng.

He placed a bag of silver on the counter and took out a hundred taels as deposit for some samples of ginseng. He explained himself thus: "My master is extremely fussy about the quality of his ginseng, and if I buy some that he's not happy with, he's sure to punish me. I loathe buying ginseng because I'm always worried about making a mistake.

"Would it be possible for me to leave this money as a deposit on a range of samples and have one of your more experienced salesmen bring them along to my master's house so that the master can examine it personally?"

The storekeeper thought this a reasonable proposition, so he accepted the deposit and instructed an experienced, middle-aged salesman to accompany the young man back to his master's with several pounds of ginseng. Just as the salesman was about to leave, the storekeeper advised him, "Be sure to keep an eye on this ginseng. Don't let anyone else get hold of it."

The young man and the salesman traveled out of the city through the Donghua Gate and eventually arrived at the steps of a mansion. The master of the house, a well-groomed man in fur whose hat bore a sapphire, was upstairs and did indeed look extremely ill.

Resting against his pillow, he addressed the salesman, "This ginseng you bear—is it of the best quality from the northeast?"

The salesman said that it was, whereupon two houseboys standing in attendance came forward and took the ginseng to the master for his perusal. He opened the bundle, packet by packet, apparently quite an expert in judging the quality of ginseng.

Before he had completed his inspection a horse-drawn carriage stopped outside. Someone obviously familiar with the household entered the hall downstairs, and the master, looking rather anxious, instructed his attendants to inform the new arrival that he was too sick to see visitors.

He then lowered his voice and said to the salesman, "This man has come to ask me for a loan. I can't let him up here now. If he sees me buying ginseng, I'll never be able to refuse him."

The shouts of the newcomer reverberated up the stairs. "Your master's just pretending to be sick! I'll bet the real reason he won't see me is that he's in bed with some luscious concubine or a young houseboy! Well, I'm going to go upstairs anyway to see for myself!"

The two attendants tried to stop him and a noisy argument ensued.

The master became even more anxious and said to the salesman in a worried whisper, "Quick, hide your ginseng! We must not let this rascal get even the slightest glimpse of it. There's a bamboo box at the foot of the bed. That should be a safe place for it."

The salesman was handed a copper padlock and key with which to lock the ginseng in the box.

"You stay here. Sit on the box and guard the ginseng. I'll go down and try to stop him."

The master staggered off down the hall and greeted the newcomer. Their relationship seemed to be fairly amicable since there was a lot of good-humored bantering. The guest, though, persisted in his request to be allowed upstairs. The master, however, continued to refuse. This point of disagreement led to a huge argument.

The guest said in anger, "You're worried that if I go upstairs I'll see all your money! You don't want to lend me any, do you? Well, I'll not be treated so callously! I'll never bother you again! Goodbye!"

The master pleaded for forgiveness and followed the guest out of the house to see him off. The attendants also appeared to have gone, since the house had fallen instantly silent.

The silence continued for quite some time while the salesman sat on the box waiting patiently for someone to return.

After a long while, the salesman's suspicions were aroused. He unlocked the box to take the ginseng back to the store but to his surprise it had disappeared. He then discovered that the box he had been sitting on had a false base. What he had assumed to be the bottom of the box was in fact the floor, whose boards opened like a trapdoor into the room below.

The noise of the argument had obviously muffled the noise of the floorboards opening, so the salesman hadn't noticed the theft of the ginseng he had been guarding so carefully.

## *Stealing a Painting*

One day a burglar sneaked into the house of a wealthy man in broad daylight, planning to steal a scroll. He had just rolled up the scroll and was about to escape when the master of the house walked in.

Realizing he was trapped, the thief, clutching the scroll, fell to his knees and pleaded, "Kind sir, I am but a poverty-stricken man with no hope for the future. I have come to you today with a portrait of my ancestor in the hope that you will exchange it for a peck of rice."

The master burst out in a sneering laugh and with an impatient flick of his hands sent the man on his way. He didn't even bother to look at the scroll.

When he walked into his hall, however, he saw that his priceless Zhao Zi'ang scroll had vanished.

# *Stealing a Pair of Boots*

One day a man wearing brand-new boots was walking around town when he was approached by another man, a complete stranger, who proceeded to bow and shake hands and chat as if he were an old friend.

Our fellow in the new boots said in a puzzled tone, "I'm terribly sorry, sir, but I don't believe we have ever met before!"

The stranger laughed testily. "So, now that you've got yourself some new boots you're too good for your old friends, eh?"

The stranger then snatched the hat from the puzzled man's head and tossed it onto the roof of a nearby building before walking off.

Our hatless man assumed that the fellow must have been drunk, and was just wondering what to do next when another fellow came towards him, saying, "That was a really nasty trick that man played on you! You really need a hat on a hot, sunny day like today, too. It'd pay to get your hat down off that roof."

The man wearing the boots replied, "You're right, but without a ladder there's really not much I can do."

His new acquaintance then made a generous offer. "Why don't you stand on my shoulders and I'll hoist you up? I'm a real do-gooder, aren't I?"

Gratefully accepting, the man with the new boots made as if to climb onto the other's back.

The kneeling man, for his part, shrugged his shoulders and turned away looking rather upset.

"Hang on a minute! Don't be in such a hurry. I know you're rather keen on that hat of yours, but what about my shirt? I'm rather keen on my shirt, too, you know, and even though your boots are pretty new they're still quite muddy. I'm sure you don't want to dirty my shirt, do you?"

This speech left the hatless man quite embarrassed, so he removed his new boots and left them on the ground in the care of his new friend.

Hoisted onto the roof in his socks, he scrambled up to retrieve his hat, but when he turned around he saw his boots disappearing down the road with the "helpful" man.

Stranded high on the roof, our bootless man was helpless, and it took ages before the people in the market came to his aid with a ladder. All assumed they had witnessed a harmless prank between friends.

By the time the truth finally emerged, the boots and the man who took them had both disappeared for good.

# *Stealing a Wall*

In the capital there lived a wealthy man who one day decided to purchase some bricks to construct a wall around his home.

He was approached by a stranger, whom we shall call Mr. X, and was told, "One of the prince's residences is currently having its outer wall replaced. Why don't you go and buy the old bricks from him?"

The wealthy man was rather suspicious of this tale and replied, "The prince surely wouldn't be interested in selling his old bricks."

"I was a bit doubtful myself, but let me reassure you," Mr. X said. "I used to serve this prince and I certainly would not lie about such a matter. Why don't you send a servant along with me, and he and I will confirm the sale with the prince himself?

"Since I will have to address the prince in Manchu, your servant won't be able to understand what is said, but he'll know the deal is clinched if the prince nods his head."

The wealthy man thought this was a sensible idea and so he sent a servant, bearing a ruler with which to measure the bricks, to accompany Mr. X. The ruler was the common measure for bricks in those days, and if you bought the bricks secondhand you could often get them for half the original price.

The small party waited outside the courthouse where the prince was in attendance, and when he finally emerged, Mr. X knelt down in front of the prince's horse and spoke in Manchu.

The prince nodded and pointed in the direction of the wall in front of his residence, saying, "You are quite welcome to measure my wall. Please go ahead."

Mr. X then took the ruler, and he and the servant began to measure the wall, both length and breadth. The wall turned out to be 177 feet long. The price was calculated to be a mere 100 cash per foot. The calculations complete, Mr. X and the servant returned and gave the wealthy man the details of the transaction.

This deal made our wealthy man very happy since he was getting his bricks for half the normal price, so he duly paid the requested amount to Mr. X. He waited for an auspicious day to construct the wall, and when that day arrived he sent his servant at the head of a team of men he had charged with the duty of pulling the wall down.

They had just begun their task when they were confronted by the prince's chief guard, who was furious at this vandalism. He immediately had the servant arrested.

When the guard interrogated the prisoner he was told, "This was done with your prince's consent." So the chief guard reported the matter to the prince, seeking confirmation.

The latter laughed when he heard the tale. "This must have something to do with that man who asked if he could measure my wall. He told me he was the servant of a Manchu nobleman who admired the design of my wall and wanted to build an identical one. I thought this was a perfectly reasonable request so I invited him to take as many measurements as he needed. I never once said I wanted to sell my wall!"

The wealthy man begged forgiveness for his blunder and pleaded for the release of his servant.

Both requests were granted, but at the cost of quite a lot of money in fees and bribes.

Mr. X was by this stage far from the district and was never located.

# *Daylight Ghosts*

There was once an extremely skillful thief by the name of Qi. So successful was he at his profession that he had accumulated tremendous wealth.

The problem was, he became increasingly worried that all these local crimes would eventually be traced back to him. So he decided as a precaution to move into a rundown old house next to the local cemetery.

One night he was visited in a dream by several ghosts. They told him, "We'll guarantee your continued prosperity if you make a few offerings to us."

In the dream Qi agreed to provide the ghosts with the requested offerings, but when he awoke he decided it had all been a load of nonsense and promptly forgot his promise.

It wasn't long before the ghosts reappeared to him in another dream. This time they said, "You promised to make the offerings to us within three days. If this promise is not fulfilled we'll come during the night and take away all your ill-gotten gains."

Now Qi was a very obstinate man and the next morning he resolved once again to ignore their requests. Qi soon fell ill and, remembering the ghosts' threat, told his wife to keep a close eye on his loot.

At noon, pieces of his hoard began to move out of the house seemingly of their own accord. Qi tried to get out of bed to halt the flow, but found that his hands and feet were tied. After every single stolen item had departed from the house, Qi's limbs were freed from their bindings and his illness instantly disappeared.

And then Qi saw the light. "Just as I had drugged people during their sleep to carry out my various burglaries, so the ghosts drugged me! Except that they did their burglary during daytime. These must be what people call 'daylight ghosts.'"

From that day forth, Qi was a reformed man who devoted his life to acts of virtue.

# *About the Translators*

**Kam Louie** is Chair of Chinese at the University of Queensland. He is the author and editor of several books on Chinese philosophy, literature, and language, including *Inheriting Tradition: Interpretations of the Classical Philosophers in Communist China 1949–1966* (1986) and *Strange Tales From Strange Lands: Stories by Zheng Wanlong* (1993).

**Louise Edwards** is lecturer in Asian Studies at Australian Catholic University (Queensland Campus). She is the author of *Men and Women in Qing China: Gender in the Red Chamber Dream* (1994) and *Recreating the Literary Canon* (1995).

Kam Louie and Louise Edwards have collaborated on a number of other projects, including compiling the *Bibliography of English Translations and Critiques of Contemporary Chinese Fiction 1945–1992* (1993).

Lightning Source UK Ltd.
Milton Keynes UK
UKHW020005021118
331627UK00025B/500/P